The Room in the Tower and Other Stories

A Supernatural Horror Story of a Haunted Space and Lingering Spirits

A Modern Translation

Adapted for the Contemporary Reader

E. F. Benson

Translated by Tim Zengerink

Table of Contents

Preface - Message to the Reader 1

Introduction 4

Preface 9

The Room in the Tower 10

The Dust-Cloud 24

Gavon's Eve 37

The Confession of Charles Linkworth 49

At Abdul Ali's Grave 69

The Shootings of Achnaleish 84

How Fear Departed from the Long Gallery 102

Caterpillars 118

The Cat 127

The Bus-Conductor 142

The Man Who Went Too Far 151

Between the Lights 175

Outside the Door 186

The Terror by Night 193

The Other Bed 201

The Thing in the Hall 209

The House with the Brick-Kiln 221

Thank You for Reading 233

Preface - Message to the Reader

What If You Could Help Rebuild the Greatest Library in Human History?

Thousands of years ago, the Library of Alexandria stood as the crown jewel of human achievement — a sanctuary where the collected wisdom of every known civilization was gathered, preserved, and shared freely.

And then, it was lost.

Through fire, conquest, and the slow erosion of time, humanity lost not just books — but ideas, dreams, discoveries, and stories that could have changed the world forever.

Today, the Library of Alexandria lives again — and you are invited to be a part of its restoration.

Our mission is simple yet profound:

To rebuild the greatest library the world has ever known, and to translate all timeless works into every language and dialect, so that no seeker of knowledge is ever left behind again.

By joining our movement to rebuild the modern Library of Alexandria, you become part of an unprecedented mission:

- **Unlimited Access to the Greatest Audiobooks & eBooks Ever Written:**

  Instantly explore thousands of legendary works—Plato, Shakespeare, Jane Austen, Leo Tolstoy, and countless more. All instantly available to read or listen, placing a complete literary universe at your fingertips.

- **Beautiful Paperback & Deluxe Editions at Printing Cost**

  Own any title as an elegant paperback, deluxe hardcover, or stunning collectible boxset—offered to you at true printing cost, delivered straight to your door. Build your personal Library of Alexandria, crafted for beauty, built for durability, and worthy of proud display.

- **Fresh Translations for Modern Readers—in Every Language & Dialect**

  Enjoy timeless masterpieces reimagined in clear, contemporary language—no more outdated phrases or obscure references. Alongside the original versions, we're tirelessly translating these classics into every language and dialect imaginable, ensuring accessibility and understanding across cultures and generations.

- **Join a Global Renaissance of Literature & Knowledge**

  You directly support expanding our library, publishing deluxe editions at true cost, translating works into all global languages, and bringing humanity's greatest stories to people everywhere. By joining today, you're not just preserving a legacy of masterpieces; you set in motion a powerful wave of literary accessibility.

Become a Torchbearer of Knowledge.

Join us for free now at **LibraryofAlexandria.com**

Together, we will ensure that the light of human wisdom never fades again.

With gratitude and a shared love of knowledge,

The Modern Library of Alexandria Team

Visit:

www.libraryofalexandria.com

Or scan the code below:

Introduction

Unspoken Fears, Hidden Spaces, and the Essence of Gothic Terror

E.F. Benson's The Room, though brief in form, stands as one of the most quietly disturbing and symbolically rich entries in the canon of supernatural fiction. Best known for his sharply satirical Mapp and Lucia novels, Benson also authored some of the finest ghost stories of the Edwardian period—stories that defied the tropes of Victorian melodrama in favor of psychological precision, atmospheric dread, and a modern sensibility attuned to the subtleties of fear. Alongside M.R. James and Algernon Blackwood, Benson shaped a distinctly British strand of ghostly fiction—one marked less by overt horror and more by suggestion, nuance, and the eerie presence of the unseen.

The Room, first published in 1912, is emblematic of this style. It offers no violent haunting, no grotesque apparitions, and no dramatic confrontation with the supernatural. Instead, it presents a minimalist, almost clinical account of terror—a tale that unfolds with hushed dread, where the fear arises not from what happens, but from what might, from what lingers just beyond perception. In a world of rational men, elegant houses, and polite conversation, The Room injects an invisible rot—a force that cannot be explained, yet cannot be ignored.

The story centers around the mysterious upstairs room in a newly acquired home. It is a room that exerts a strange psychological pressure on those who enter it, even for a moment. Several characters—independently and without collusion—begin to sense that something in the room is wrong. There is no noise. No movement. Only silence, emptiness, and a pervasive sense of malevolence. Over time, the room's influence grows. People begin to avoid it. Some refuse to speak of it. And one, in the end, is undone by it. In this simple premise, Benson constructs a masterclass in slow-building terror—a study in how space, silence, and suggestion can induce existential fear.

This introduction explores The Room as both a gothic artifact and a psychological case study. We will examine Benson's minimalist approach to the supernatural, the use of architectural space as a metaphor for the subconscious, and the story's broader philosophical implications about dread, sanity, and the unnameable forces that lurk within us. As we shall see, The Room is not just haunted by a spirit—it is haunted by something older, something more primal: the human mind's inability to face the void without flinching.

The Architecture of Fear: Spatial Dread and the Unnamed Horror

At the heart of The Room is its titular space—an empty, unfurnished room that holds no visible threat but exerts a profound psychic weight on those who enter it. Benson, like M.R. James before him, understood that the most terrifying spaces are not those filled with gore or spectacle, but those that remain stubbornly blank. The horror of the room is that it does nothing—yet everyone feels it.

The room functions as a gothic device in the purest sense. In traditional gothic fiction, the haunted room or forbidden chamber is often the site of revelation—where secrets are exposed or transgressions are punished. In The Room, however, there is no such resolution. The space is empty, yet it radiates something—some unseen force or moral infection that preys on the mind. The narrator, a rational man of intellect and culture, begins the story with detached amusement. But even he cannot maintain this stance for long. The room gets to him. Not through events, but through presence.

This dread is spatial rather than narrative. Benson uses the architecture of the house—its clean rooms, its pleasant furnishings, its quiet elegance—to frame the horror more starkly. The room is just another room, and that is what makes it so disturbing. It should be safe. It should be ordinary. But it is not. Something is off. And no one can say why.

In this, Benson plays on a uniquely modern anxiety: the idea that horror can exist anywhere, without cause or context. The supernatural no longer needs backstory or myth. It can dwell in an unused bedroom, behind a closed door, for no reason at all. This notion—that malevolence can be ambient, arbitrary, and undetectable—is at the heart of Benson's brilliance.

The Mind as Haunted House: Psychological Descent and Existential Dread

While the story's surface concerns a haunted room, its deeper subject is the haunting of the self. What makes The Room so effective is its psychological realism. The fear experienced by the characters is not theatrical; it is intimate, internal, and largely unspoken. They do not scream or faint. They withdraw. They fall silent. They avoid the room with quiet desperation, as if naming the fear would give it power.

The narrator's arc is especially significant. He begins as a skeptical observer, amused by the irrational fears of others. But gradually, the room begins to work on him—not with visions or threats, but with atmosphere. His inner monologue becomes hesitant. His confidence falters. He begins to question his senses. In this shift, we see the true subject of the story emerge: the collapse of certainty, the disintegration of self-assurance in the face of nothing.

This is not horror as external threat. It is horror as epistemological failure—a breakdown in the narrator's ability to trust his own perception. He cannot prove that the room is dangerous. No harm has occurred. Yet he feels the danger as keenly as a physical wound. Benson captures this unraveling with perfect restraint, allowing the reader to inhabit the narrator's slow descent into self-doubt.

By the end, the story offers no closure. The room is not exorcised. No explanation is given. The narrator simply leaves. And in that choice—to flee rather than confront—we are left with a chilling truth: sometimes, we do not want answers. We want distance. The most terrifying rooms are not those we explore. They are the ones we avoid.

E.F. Benson and the Modern Gothic Sensibility

E.F. Benson (1867–1940) was a writer of remarkable range, best known for his satirical novels but equally gifted in the realm of supernatural fiction. Alongside his brothers Arthur and Robert, both of whom were literary figures in their own right, Benson helped define a new kind of ghost story for the Edwardian age—one that moved away from the melodrama of Victorian fiction and toward psychological subtlety and modern ambiguity.

In stories like The Room in the Tower, Caterpillars, and The Face, Benson explored terror through atmosphere, understatement, and suggestion. He was less interested in demons or ghosts than in the idea of presence—something unseen but felt, something that changes the way a space is perceived. In The Room, this aesthetic reaches its purest form. There is no ghost. There is no origin. There is only dread. And dread, for Benson, is enough.

This minimalist approach would prove deeply influential. Writers like Shirley Jackson, Robert Aickman, and even Stephen King owe a debt to Benson's economy of language and psychological focus. In many ways, The Room anticipates modern horror's shift toward interiority—the idea that what terrifies us most is not what lurks outside, but what dwells within.

Benson also deserves credit for his moral neutrality. Unlike many of his contemporaries, he does not moralize or punish. He does not explain or resolve. He allows fear to exist as a condition of being, not as a consequence of sin. This existential framing places him closer to modernist thinkers than to traditional gothic fabulists. In The Room, horror is not a disruption of order—it is a glimpse of the void behind it.

The Room is, ultimately, a story about what we cannot explain. It is a meditation on unease, on the silence that surrounds fear, and on the human tendency to fill that silence with the worst of ourselves. It is a story that lingers—not because of what happens, but because of what doesn't.

And that, perhaps, is the truest haunting of all.

Preface

These stories were written to give readers a few good shivers. The hope is that if someone happens to read them late at night, when the house is quiet and the darkness has settled in, they might find themselves glancing into the corners of the room—just to make sure nothing strange is hiding in the shadows. After all, that's the true purpose of ghost stories and tales about unseen, mysterious forces: to make people feel a little uneasy. The writer sincerely hopes to give readers a few moments of real discomfort.

Some of these stories were first published in different magazines, while the rest are brand new. One story, "The Man Who Went Too Far," later grew into a full novel called The Angel of Pain.

E. F. BENSON.

The Room in the Tower

Most people who dream a lot have probably had at least one experience where something they dreamed about later happened in real life. But to me, that doesn't seem strange at all. It would actually be stranger if it never happened, since our dreams usually involve people and places we already know, things that could easily appear in our waking lives. Of course, dreams often get interrupted by weird or impossible events that would never happen in real life. But just by the law of chances, it makes sense that a dream could sometimes come true.

Not long ago, I had one of those dreams come true — although I didn't think it was anything special or supernatural. Here's what happened:

I have a friend who lives in another country and writes me a letter about every two weeks. So after two weeks, either consciously or without realizing it, I start expecting a letter. One night last week, I dreamed that I was heading upstairs to get dressed for dinner when I heard the postman knock at the door. I changed direction, went downstairs, and among the mail, I found a letter from my friend. That part made sense. But then the dream got strange: when I opened the letter, inside was the ace of diamonds playing card, with a note from my friend saying, "I'm sending you this for safe keeping. You know it's risky to keep aces in Italy."

The next night, just as I was about to go upstairs, I heard the postman's knock for real. I went down and found a letter from my friend, just like in my dream. Of course, the ace of diamonds wasn't inside. If it had been, I might have thought something mysterious was going on. But since it wasn't, I just saw it as a normal coincidence. I had probably been expecting a letter, and my dream reflected that. Likewise, my friend probably thought it was about time he wrote to me again.

Still, sometimes things happen in dreams that are harder to explain — and that brings me to the story I'm about to tell, which I can't explain at all. It came out of nowhere, and then disappeared just as mysteriously.

All my life, I've been someone who dreams a lot. Most mornings I wake up remembering at least one dream, and often it feels like I've had incredible adventures all night long. Usually, these dreams are pleasant, even if they're unimportant. But once in a while, something different happens.

I was about sixteen years old when a certain dream first came to me. It happened like this:

The dream began with me being dropped off at the door of a big red-brick house. I knew somehow that I was going to stay there. A servant opened the door and told me that tea was being served outside in the garden. He led me through a dark, wood-paneled hallway with a huge open fireplace, and out onto a bright green lawn surrounded by flower beds.

Around a tea table sat a small group of people. I didn't recognize anyone except one boy, Jack Stone, a schoolmate I barely knew and didn't even like much. He introduced me to his parents and his two sisters. I was surprised to find myself there, especially since Jack had left our school almost a year earlier.

The afternoon was extremely hot, and the air felt heavy and suffocating. Across the lawn was a red-brick wall with an iron gate in the center, and just beyond the gate stood a walnut tree. We sat in the shade of the house, facing a row of tall windows. Through them, I could see a dining table covered in gleaming glass and silver.

This side of the house was very long, and at one end stood a three-story tower that looked older than the rest of the building.

For a while, no one said a word. Then Mrs. Stone broke the silence by telling me, "Jack will show you your room. I've given you the room in the tower."

Hearing this filled me with dread, although I didn't know why. Somehow, deep down, I had expected to be given that room — and I sensed that something terrible was waiting there. Jack stood up at once, and without speaking, I followed him.

We walked back through the hall and up a huge oak staircase that twisted and turned. At the top, we came to a small landing with two doors. Jack opened one of them for me but didn't come in. He simply closed the door behind me.

The moment I stepped inside, I knew I had been right. Something awful was in that room. Terror flooded through me — the kind of raw fear you feel only in nightmares — and I woke up, gasping in panic.

The dream — or different versions of it — kept coming back to me every so often for fifteen years. Most of the time, it was the same: I would arrive at the house, tea would be set out on the lawn, the terrible silence would hang over us, then Mrs. Stone would say those dreaded words, and I would follow Jack Stone up to the room in the tower, where a feeling of horror always overwhelmed me. I never actually saw what was in the room.

Sometimes the dream changed a little. Once in a while, instead of tea on the lawn, we would be sitting at dinner inside the house — the same dining room I had seen through the windows on my first visit.

No matter where we were, though, the silence and the heavy feeling of fear were always there. And always, eventually, Mrs. Stone would break the silence by saying, "Jack will show you your room: I have given you the room in the tower." Then, no matter what, I would have to follow him up the twisting oak staircase to that dreaded room.

Other times, the dream would find me playing cards in a drawing room that was dazzlingly bright with huge chandeliers. I never knew what game we were playing. What I do remember is struggling to see my cards clearly, even though the room was full of light. All the cards were black — there were no red suits — and some were entirely black with no markings at all. I hated those cards and feared them.

As the dream repeated over the years, I became familiar with more parts of the house. There was a dark smoking-room beyond the drawing-room, down a hallway with a green baize door. Every time I went there, I would pass someone in the doorway — someone I could never see clearly.

The people in the dream changed too, as if they were real and aging along with time. Mrs. Stone, who had been black-haired when I first saw her, grew gray and moved more slowly when she said, "Jack will show you your room." Jack himself became a young man with a brown mustache and a sickly look. One of the sisters disappeared from the dream altogether, and I somehow understood she had gotten married.

Then, for more than six months, I didn't dream about the tower at all. I hoped it meant the dream had finally ended, because I had come to dread it deeply. But one night it returned.

That night, I was once again brought out onto the lawn for tea. Mrs. Stone wasn't there, and everyone else was dressed in black. My heart lifted — maybe this time I wouldn't have to sleep in the tower room. I felt so relieved that I talked and laughed, something I had never done in the dream before. But even then, the others stayed silent, just looking at each other when they thought I wasn't watching. Slowly, my relief faded, and a sense of terrible fear settled over me as the light dimmed.

Suddenly, I heard Mrs. Stone's voice — even though she wasn't there — saying, "Jack will show you your room: I have given you the room in the tower." The voice came from near the gate in the red-brick wall, and when I looked up, I saw the grass outside the gate was covered with gravestones. A strange gray light shone from them. On the nearest stone, I could clearly read the words: "In evil memory of Julia Stone."

As usual, Jack stood up, and I followed him through the hall and up the twisting staircase. This time it was even darker than before, and when I entered the room, I could barely make out the shapes of the familiar furniture. A terrible smell of decay filled the air. Overwhelmed by horror, I woke up screaming.

The dream — with all its slight changes and developments — kept haunting me for fifteen years. Sometimes I dreamed it for two or three nights in a row. Once there was a break of six months. But overall, I would say I dreamed it at least once a month.

It had all the marks of a nightmare. It always ended with a terror that didn't lessen over time, but seemed to grow even worse. There was also a strange, frightening consistency to it: the people grew older, just like they would in real life. Marriages happened. Deaths happened. After Mrs. Stone died in the dream, I never saw her again — only heard her voice telling me about the room in the tower. Whether we were drinking tea on the lawn or sitting inside, I could always see her gravestone standing just outside the iron gate.

The married daughter sometimes appeared again, always silent and accompanied by a man I assumed was her husband. Everyone in that family, whether alive or dead, was silent.

Because the dream repeated so often, I stopped thinking much about it while I was awake. I never saw Jack Stone again in real life. I never came across a house that looked like the one from my dream.

And then, something unexpected happened.

I had been staying in London that year until the end of July, and during the first week of August, I went to visit a friend who had rented a house for the summer near Ashdown Forest in Sussex. I left London early because John Clinton, my friend, was meeting me at Forest Row Station. We planned to spend the day golfing before heading to his house in the evening. He had his car with him, and around five in the afternoon, after a great day, we started the ten-mile drive home.

Since it was still early, we decided to skip tea at the clubhouse and have it when we got back. As we drove, the weather, which had been hot but fresh, suddenly felt heavy and oppressive. I felt that strange, uneasy feeling I usually get before a thunderstorm. John didn't notice it; he thought I was just sulking because I had lost both my matches. Later events proved I was right, though the coming storm wasn't the only cause of my growing uneasiness.

We drove through deep lanes with high banks on either side. Before long, I dozed off and didn't wake up until the car stopped. With a sudden jolt of fear — but mostly curiosity — I realized I was standing in front of the house from my dreams.

Still half-dazed, I walked with John through a low, oak-paneled hall and out onto a lawn where tea was laid out under the shadow of the house. The lawn was surrounded by flower beds, and beyond a red-brick wall with a gate stood a patch of rough grass with a walnut tree. The front of the house was very long, and at one end rose a three-story tower that looked much older than the rest of the building.

At that point, though, the dream and real life stopped matching. Instead of the silent, frightening family from my dreams, there were lots of cheerful people I knew. And even though the scene was so familiar, I didn't feel any fear now — just intense curiosity about what would happen next.

Tea went on happily. After a while, Mrs. Clinton stood up, and even before she spoke, I somehow knew what she was about to say. She turned to me and said:

"Jack will show you your room: I have given you the room in the tower."

For a moment, the old terror from my dreams gripped me. But it passed quickly, and all I felt was burning curiosity.

John turned to me.

"Your room's right at the top," he said. "But I think you'll be comfortable. We're packed full. Want to come see it now? By the way, you were right — looks like we're going to get a storm. It's gotten really dark."

I followed him through the hall and up the staircase — the very one I knew so well from my dreams. He opened the door, and I stepped into the room. Once again, sheer terror grabbed me. I didn't even know what I was afraid of — just that I was. Then, like remembering a name you had forgotten, it came to me: I was afraid of Mrs. Stone, the woman whose grave with the words "In evil memory" I had so often seen from the window.

But just as quickly, the fear left, and I stood calmly in the room I knew so well from my dreams: the room in the tower.

I looked around with a strange feeling that it belonged to me. Everything was exactly as it had been in my dreams. To the left of the door was the bed against the wall; along the same wall were a fireplace and a small bookcase. Across from the door were two lattice-paned windows with a dressing table between them. Along the fourth wall were a washstand and a big cupboard. My luggage had already been unpacked — my clothes neatly laid out on the washstand and the bed.

Then, with a sudden chill, I noticed two things I had never seen in my dreams: a life-sized oil painting of Mrs. Stone and a black-and-white sketch of Jack Stone. The drawing of Jack showed him just as I had dreamed him a week earlier — a secretive, unpleasant-looking man of about thirty. His picture was hung between the windows, staring straight at the portrait of Mrs. Stone, which hung beside the bed.

When I looked at Mrs. Stone's portrait, the old horror washed over me again. She looked just as she had in my dreams — old, with white hair, yet somehow full of a terrifying, evil energy. Her narrow, leering eyes, her twisted smile, even her hands, clenched with secret glee — everything about her face radiated some wicked, hidden laughter. I leaned closer to the painting and saw it was signed: "Julia Stone by Julia Stone."

Just then, there was a knock, and John Clinton came in.

"Got everything you need?" he asked.

"More than I want," I said, pointing to the painting.

He laughed.

"Hard-faced old lady. She painted herself too, if I remember. Didn't flatter herself much, did she?"

"But don't you see?" I said. "It's hardly human. It looks like a witch — or something worse."

John looked again.

"Yeah, it's not exactly cozy," he agreed. "Might give you nightmares. Want me to have it taken down?"

"I really would," I said.

John rang for a servant, and together they took the heavy painting down and carried it out onto the landing, setting it face against the wall.

"By Jove, she's heavy!" John said, wiping his forehead. "Wonder if she had a heavy conscience too."

I had noticed how unusually heavy the painting was. I was about to say something when I looked down at my hand — it was covered in blood.

"I must have scratched myself," I said.

John glanced at his own hand and gave a small exclamation.

"Same here!"

The footman, too, took out a handkerchief and wiped his hand — it was stained with blood as well.

John and I went back into the tower room and washed our hands. But there were no cuts or scratches on either of us.

We didn't mention it again. Somehow, without saying anything, we both seemed to agree it was better not to talk about it. Deep down, I think we both had the same chilling thought — and neither of us wanted to put it into words.

The air grew even hotter and heavier after dinner, since the storm we had expected still hadn't broken. Most of us, including John Clinton and me, sat outside on the path along the lawn where we had tea earlier. The night was completely dark, with no moon or stars visible through the thick clouds. Little by little, people began heading off — the women went up to bed, the men drifted to the smoking or billiard rooms — until by eleven o'clock only John and I were left. I had thought all evening that he seemed troubled, and once we were alone, he spoke up.

"The man who helped us move the painting had blood on his hand too. Did you notice?" he said. "I asked him if he had cut himself, but he couldn't find any mark. So where did the blood come from?"

I had forced myself all evening not to think about that strange event, and I didn't want to be reminded of it just before bed.

"I don't know," I said. "And honestly, I don't care, as long as that portrait of Julia Stone is nowhere near my bed."

John stood up.

"But it's strange," he said. "And now, you'll see something even stranger."

His dog, an Irish terrier, had come out of the house while we were talking. The door behind us was open, and a bright strip of light shone across the lawn to the iron gate by the walnut tree. I noticed the dog was stiff with fear — his fur bristled, his lips curled back to show his teeth, and he was growling low in his throat. He didn't seem to see either of us. Instead, he stiffly walked across the lawn to the gate. He stood there a moment, staring through the bars, still growling, but then suddenly gave a loud howl and ran back to the house, crouching low as he moved.

"He does that half a dozen times a day," John said. "He sees something out there he hates and fears."

Curious, I walked to the gate and looked out. I saw something moving on the grass. Then I heard a sound I couldn't place at first — until I realized it was the purring of a cat. I struck a match and saw a big blue Persian cat, walking around in a tight circle just outside the gate, tail high like a flag. Its eyes shone brightly, and every now and then it bent down to sniff the grass.

I laughed.

"So that's the end of the mystery," I said. "It's just a cat having a party all by itself."

"That's Darius," John said. "He spends half the day and all night there. But that doesn't explain the dog's terror. Toby and Darius are best friends. So why is the cat so happy while the dog is terrified?"

At that moment, I remembered the dream — the graveyard just beyond the gate, with the tombstone marked "In evil memory of Julia Stone" — and felt a shiver run through me. But before I could say anything, the rain came down suddenly and heavily, as if a tap had been turned on. At the same moment, the cat squeezed through the bars of the gate and ran to the house. It sat in the doorway, staring eagerly out into the storm. When John tried to push it inside, it hissed and swatted at him.

Despite the strange events — the bloody hands, the terrified dog, the eerie cat — I wasn't afraid. Without the painting in my room, I found no reason to be alarmed. Feeling sleepy, I went to bed, thinking about it all with more curiosity than fear. The last thing I noticed before blowing out the candle was the empty spot where the portrait had been — the wallpaper there was still dark red, while the rest of the room had faded.

I blew out the candle and fell asleep immediately.

I woke up just as suddenly. I sat straight up, feeling sure that a bright light had just flashed in my face, even though the room was now completely dark. I knew exactly where I was — in the dreaded room from my dreams — but nothing in those dreams had prepared me for the terror that now gripped me. Thunder crashed overhead, but even though I told myself it must have been lightning that woke me, it didn't calm my racing heart. I felt something in the room with me. Instinctively, I reached out my right hand toward the wall to push it away — and my fingers touched the edge of a picture frame hanging there.

I jumped out of bed, knocking over the little table beside it. I heard my watch, my matches, and my candle fall to the floor. Before I could light anything, another lightning flash lit up the room — and I saw it. Hanging above my bed again was the portrait of Mrs. Stone.

But worse, at the foot of my bed stood a figure in a clinging white garment, stained and mouldy. It was her — the face from the painting.

Thunder rolled again. As the sound died away, I heard soft, eager breathing moving closer. A wave of rotting, sickening smell filled the air. Then something cold and clammy touched the side of my neck, and the breathing came right against my ear. And then the voice — the voice I already knew — whispered:

"I knew you would come to the room in the tower. I've waited for you. Tonight, I will feast... and soon, we will feast together."

The terror that had frozen me broke at last. I struck out with my arms and kicked, and something small and soft fell beside me with a thud. I stumbled forward, nearly tripping over it, but managed to find the door handle. I yanked the door open, slammed it behind me, and ran onto the landing.

At that moment, John Clinton, holding a candle, came running up the stairs.

“What is it?” he cried. “I heard a crash — and—good heavens, there’s blood on your shoulder!”

Later, he told me I was swaying on my feet, white as a ghost, with a bloody handprint on my shoulder — like a hand had grabbed me.

"It’s in there," I said hoarsely, pointing back to the door. "The portrait... and her..."

John laughed nervously.

"My dear fellow, it’s just a nightmare," he said.

He brushed past me and pushed the door open. I couldn’t follow. I was paralyzed with terror.

“God, what a stench!” he said from inside.

There was a moment of silence. Then he reappeared, as pale as me, and shut the door quickly behind him.

"Yes, the painting’s there," he said, "and on the floor... there’s something... something covered in dirt, like a body from a grave. Come away. Quick, come away."

I barely remember how we got downstairs. I was shaking so badly that John had to guide my feet down each step. He kept glancing nervously up the stairs. Finally, we reached his dressing room, and I told him everything.

The rest of the story can be told quickly. Some of you might already have guessed what it was, if you remember the strange incident at West Fawley eight years ago — when a woman who had committed suicide was buried three times, but each time her coffin forced itself back up through the ground.

Finally, to stop the rumors, they buried her elsewhere — just outside the gate of the house where she had lived... the house where she had killed herself, in the room at the top of the tower.

Her name was Julia Stone.

Later, they secretly dug up the body again — and found the coffin full of blood.

The Dust-Cloud

The big French windows were open onto the lawn, and after dinner, a few of the guests who were staying with the Combe-Martins at the end of August wandered outside to look at the sea. The moon was just rising, large and low, casting a pale gold path across the water. Some of the others, less interested in moonlight, had gone off to find a game of bridge or billiards. Coffee had been served right after dessert, and, following the house's relaxed tradition, everyone stayed or left as they pleased—smoking, sipping port, or doing nothing at all.

That evening, Harry Combe-Martin and I ended up alone in the dining room because we were deep in a conversation about cars—specifically, the impressive new six-cylinder Napier that Harry had recently bought. The rest of the group had been bored and left us to it. Harry proudly talked about his car, mentioning that he planned to drive me to lunch at a friend's house near Hunstanton the next day. He added that we didn't even need an early start—eighty miles was no big deal, and there were no police traps to worry about.

"These big cars are strange things," Harry said as we got up. "Sometimes it feels less like a machine and more like a living creature. It's like having a thoroughbred horse with a really fine mouth."

"And the moods of a thoroughbred too?" I joked.

"No, thank goodness," he said. "It has a great temper. Some cars get moody if you slow them down or stop them when they're running well. But mine's steady."

He paused before ringing the bell.

"Take Guy Elphinstone's car, for example. That thing was a bad-tempered beast."

"What kind was it?" I asked.

"A twenty-five horsepower Amédée. Those are high-strung cars, too delicate—no strong bones. And a little bone is good for the nerves. That car liked running over chickens or rabbits—maybe more because of Guy's temper than the car's, but still. He paid for it though—paid dearly. Did you know him?"

"No, but I recognize the name. Didn't he run over a child?"

"Yes," Harry said, "and smashed into his own park gates afterward."

"He died, didn't he?"

"Instantly. The car was just a pile of wreckage. There's an odd story about it too—something up your alley."

"Ghosts?" I asked.

"Yes, the ghost of his motorcar. Sounds too modern to be true, doesn't it?"

"What's the story?" I asked.

"Well, his estate was outside the village of Bircham, about ten miles from Norwich. There's a long straight stretch of road where he ran over the child, and just a few hundred yards further is a sharp turn into his park gates. A month or two after the accident, an old villager swore he saw a motorcar speeding silently down that road, disappearing at the park gates—which were shut at the time. Soon after, someone else said he heard a motor race past, followed by a horrible scream—but saw nothing."

"The scream's creepy," I said.

"Oh, I get what you mean!" said Harry. "I was only thinking of his car's siren. Guy had a siren attached to his exhaust—it made an awful, scared-sounding wail. It always gave me the creeps."

"And that's the whole story?" I asked. "One man sees a silent car, another hears an invisible one?"

Harry flicked his cigarette ash into the fireplace.

"Hardly," he said. "Half a dozen people claim to have seen or heard something. It's a well-supported story."

"Yes, probably edited over a few drinks at the pub," I said.

"Well, none of them will go near that road after dark anymore. The lodge-keeper even quit. He said he kept hearing a motor stop and honk outside the lodge at night, but when he ran out to look, there was never anything there."

"And his wife?" I asked.

"She heard a child screaming and would rush to check if their kids were safe. And the children—"

"What about them?" I asked.

"They kept asking their mother who the little girl was that walked up and down the road, refusing to speak or play with them."

"That's a lot of different stories," I said. "Everybody seems to have a different experience."

"That's exactly what makes the story good," Harry said. "I don't really believe in ghosts, but if they exist—and if Guy's death and the child's stirred them up—then it makes sense that different people would experience different things. One hears the car, another sees it. One hears the child, another sees her. Doesn't that seem more believable?"

I had to admit that this was a new idea for me—and the more I thought about it, the more reasonable it sounded. If only a few people can see or hear ghosts, it makes sense that some would be more sensitive to sight, others to sound.

"Yes, it makes sense," I said. "Can't you take me there?"

"Sure, if you can stay till Friday. We can go Thursday night after the others leave."

"I can't stay that long," I said. "I have to leave Thursday. Couldn't we stop by on the way to or from Hunstanton tomorrow?"

"No, it's thirty miles out of the way. Plus, if we wait for it to get dark at Bircham, we wouldn't get home until midnight—and I have guests to host."

"So everything only happens after dark?" I asked. "That makes it less exciting. Like a séance where they turn out all the lights."

"Well, the accident happened at night," he said. "Maybe that has something to do with it, though I don't know the rules."

I had another question in mind, but I didn't want to ask it directly. I wanted to find out without making it obvious.

"I don't know much about cars either," I said. "I didn't quite understand when you said Guy Elphinstone's car acted like an angry beast that liked running over rabbits and chickens. But later you hinted that maybe it was Guy, not the car, who was bad-tempered. Did he get angry when he had to slow down?"

"It made him crazy if it happened too often," said Harry. "I'll never forget one drive with him — there were hay carts and baby carriages every few hundred yards. It was awful, like being stuck with a madman. And when we finally got to his gate, his dog came running out to meet him. He didn't even try to avoid it—worse than that, he aimed right at it, grinding his teeth with rage. I never rode with him again."

Harry paused, guessing what I might be thinking.

"I say, you mustn't think—you mustn't think—" he began.

"No, of course not," I said quickly.

Harry's house was perched near the sandy cliffs of the Suffolk coast, where the sea was always eating away at the land. Far out under the water lay what used to be Dunwich, once the second-biggest port in England. Now, only ruins of one of its seven great churches remained, already half lost to the crumbling cliff and the sea's relentless pull. The graveyard around the church had mostly collapsed too, so from the edge of the cliff, you could see bones sticking out of the sand, like straws in glass, just as Dante once described.

Maybe it was remembering that grim sight from the afternoon, or maybe it was Harry's story troubling my mind, or maybe it was just the sharp, bracing sea air after coming from the sleepy Norfolk Broads—but whatever the reason, I couldn't sleep that night. As soon as I blew out the light and got into bed, it felt like all the lights inside my mind turned on, leaving me wide awake.

I tried every trick to fall asleep: counting forward and backward, imagining sheep jumping through a gap in a hedge, playing games of noughts and crosses with myself, even mapping out rows of tennis courts. But nothing worked. Every time I repeated these boring exercises, I only got more alert. I didn't keep doing them because I hoped for sleep anymore, but because I didn't want my mind to wander to darker thoughts—about those bones on the cliff, or about the question I had promised Harry not to dwell on. I kept my mind busy with nonsense, like shouting over a voice I didn't want to hear.

But little by little, even that became impossible. My mind refused to keep up the game. And in a flash, I found myself thinking not about the bones, but about the thing I had promised to avoid: what Harry had really meant when he warned me not to think about it. Surely, it was because he had reached a terrible conclusion himself—and didn't want me to reach it too.

The whole question of haunted places—houses, graveyards, scenes of tragedy—has always seemed to me neither completely proven nor completely disproven. Since the earliest times, people have believed that the place where a crime happened could be haunted—sometimes by the one who committed it, searching for peace but finding none, sometimes by the victim's spirit, crying out for justice.

Sure, the old men's stories from the village pub about ghostly cars and invisible sounds weren't very reliable. But the children's questions stuck with me. How could kids make up a silent, unfriendly little girl walking by, refusing to speak or play with them? Maybe it was just a real but sulky child. Maybe. But maybe not.

After turning that over in my mind, I couldn't help thinking about the harder question—the one about Guy Elphinstone. Had the death of the child really been an accident, something he couldn't have helped? Or had he, angry and impatient after being slowed down all day, seen the child in the road and simply not cared—just as he hadn't cared when he ran down animals or even his own dog?

And what must have gone through his mind in the awful moment between the child's death and his own? If he had felt remorse, true bitter regret, surely he would have stopped. But he hadn't. He had raced forward even faster, straight into his own gate, smashing the car into splinters.

And then came the most terrible question of all: after killing the child, had he felt some twisted, savage joy—and rushed on to his own death filled with a kind of evil triumph?

In my mind, the horror of it stood out sharp and clear—like the bones jutting out from the sand cliff into the night.

The pale, tired light of early morning had turned the window shades into glowing squares before I finally fell asleep. When I woke up, the servant was already in the room, quickly pulling up the blinds and letting the bright, calm August morning flood the space. Sunlight, a fresh sea breeze, the scent of flowers, and the songs of birds poured through the open windows. All of it felt so comforting, sweeping away the dark, heavy feelings that had haunted me during the night. I thought about those restless hours the way a traveler thinks of rough storms at sea once he's safely on land — no longer troubled by them now that they were just a memory.

I also felt a real sense of relief knowing I wouldn't be visiting that strange and unsettling place after all. Today's drive, as Harry had said, would take us nowhere near Bircham, and tomorrow I would be heading straight to the station to leave. A true seeker of the supernatural might have regretted missing the chance to visit Bircham at night and see whether those ghost stories had any truth to them. But I felt no such regret. Bircham had already given me one sleepless night, and I knew I had no real desire to go there, even though yesterday I had said otherwise. In the bright sunlight and fresh sea breeze, I felt healthy, happy to be alive—and very glad not to be going near Bircham. My curiosity could stay unsatisfied.

Around eleven o'clock, the motor car rolled around, and we set off. Harry and his cousin Mrs. Morrison sat comfortably together in the big back seat, while I sat next to the driver, lost in a kind of trance of excitement and happiness. These were still the early days of automobiles, when they seemed filled with romance and adventure. I didn't want to drive—I didn't even want Harry to drive—because driving takes so much focus that you can't really enjoy the ride. Loving cars is a passion, almost like a love for music or math. Some people ride in cars all the time and feel nothing special, while others, who rarely get the chance, feel it deeply.

The love of speed is at the heart of it—the thrill of rushing through the world, whether on a horse, skates, a bicycle, or hitting a ball in sports. But you have to really feel the speed, like sitting up front on a train, not tucked away behind closed windows. Now add to that thrill the feeling of controlling that speed with just a small lever and steering wheel. As Harry had said, it's like holding the reins of a powerful, wild horse. The motor feeds itself with fire, greedily drinking fuel and roaring to life, racing forward as if tearing the road open ahead of it. Yet with just a touch, you could make it fly faster—or slow to a stroll.

And always, the engine loved to run. You'd let it lift its voice and warn others with its hooter so you wouldn't need to slow down. If that wasn't enough, it had a wild, high-pitched scream that echoed down the lanes. Riding in such a car was like diving deep into the sea—you were isolated but thrilled, racing ahead with only the rushing air and the road stretched out in front of you. Around you were the great shining headlights, the fenders like ear-flaps, and the long sleek hood covering the beast's fiery heart, all carrying you up hills and down valleys as if some new force of nature, stronger even than gravity, was pushing you forward.

For the first hour, the pure joy of it all was mine—joy so intense that any description is like comparing a still pond to a rushing mountain stream. The road rose and fell in front of us like a switchback, and the car raced downhill in silence, then hummed and surged up the next hill without slowing. From my seat, I could control the car's voice, sounding the horn to warn a pony-cart ahead or using the high scream if needed.

Once, we came to a crossing, and the car seemed to say, "Look how careful I am," slowing itself almost to a stroll. Later, a brave little puppy staggered into the road, and the car seemed to growl kindly, warning it, "Run home, little one!" When the puppy didn't listen, the car slowed even more and gave a friendly "Whoof!" Then, as the puppy darted safely into the hedge, the car picked up speed again, laughing to itself as the wind shrieked and whistled around us once more.

I think Napoleon once said that the strength of an army lies in its feet — and that's true for our machine, too. There was a loud bang, and within thirty seconds, we came to a complete stop. Something was wrong with the machine's front left "foot," and the driver said, "Yes, sir — it's burst."

We took off the damaged tire and put on a new one, which had never been used before. We lifted the foot with a jack while we worked, and laced the new tire tight with a pump. It took exactly twenty-five minutes. After that, the machine started up again and seemed almost eager, like it was saying, "Let me run! Oh, let me run!" And for fifteen miles along a straight, empty road, it did just that. I timed how fast we went but decided not to share the numbers — just in case the police ever asked.

After that, the excitement faded. We were supposed to reach Hunstanton by lunchtime, but instead, we were fixing our fourth flat tire at 1:45 p.m., still twenty-five miles away. This time, a sharp piece of flint, less than an inch long and barely weighing anything, had caused the damage — even though we weighed two tons. It felt unfair. So we stopped at a little inn for lunch. During the meal, the experts had a serious talk, and here's what they decided:

We had run out of spare tires. The front left tire had burst once and been punctured once (which used up two socks and one tire). The back left tire was even worse — it had burst twice (meaning two socks and two tires). We didn't know if Hunstanton had a proper store, but there was a big general shop in King's Lynn, which wasn't too far away.

The driver also said something was wrong with the ignition — the "spoon," as he called it — and he wasn't sure what exactly. So, it made more sense to head for King's Lynn instead of Hunstanton, especially since lunch was already behind us. We all quietly hoped we would make it.

The last spare tire held up, the ignition worked again, and we rolled smoothly into King's Lynn. I vaguely heard that we would take a different route back, but honestly, I was so caught up in the fresh air and the ride that I didn't care where we were going. One thing I should point out: while we were in King's Lynn and on the road afterward, Bircham never crossed my mind. If I later had strange visions, they weren't because I had been thinking about Bircham. All I knew was that we had gone a bit out of our way to reach the garage. Harry even told me he didn't know where the road would lead.

Everything after this is just a simple record of what happened — though to me, a curious student of strange events, it's worth noting.

While we waited, we had tea at a hotel that looked out over a big, empty square surrounded by houses. After tea, we waited a long time for our car to be ready. Then the phone rang — it was the garage, asking for "the gentleman with the motorcar." Since Harry had gone off to buy a newspaper with news about the latest Test Match, I answered the call. What I heard wasn't good: the ignition was badly broken, and maybe they could fix it in an hour. It was around six-thirty in the evening, and we were seventy-eight miles away from Dunwich.

Harry came back shortly after, and I told him what they said. He shrugged and said, "Then we won't get back until way after dinner. We might as well have stayed out to look for your ghost!"

As I said before, Bircham wasn't even on my mind. Harry's joke even suggested we weren't passing through it.

One hour turned into an hour and a half. Then, finally, the car came roaring around the corner, ready to go. We climbed in.

"Step on it, Jack," Harry told the driver. "The roads will be empty. You should turn on the lights right away."

Jack did just that. The headlights lit up the road ahead, and we sped off. Jack drove fast but carefully — he never took any unnecessary risks. When the road was clear, he let the machine fly as fast as it could go. The headlights turned the road into daylight, and the dark countryside around us looked like something out of a fairy tale. Hares darted out from the roadside and raced ahead of us before veering away just in time. Moths fluttered across the beams, and the miles seemed to disappear behind us.

It happened while we were going full speed — a strange, simple moment that still puzzles me.

I was in charge of the horn and the siren. We were racing down a long, downhill stretch when suddenly I saw a thick cloud of dust ahead. I immediately knew what it meant: something big and fast was ahead of us, going the same direction. If it had been coming toward us, we would have seen the car before we hit the dust. And if it had been something slow, like a horse cart, it wouldn't have raised so much dust.

Whatever it was, it wasn't moving as fast as we were — because we crashed into its dust cloud all at once.

I shouted, "Slow down! Hit the brakes! There's something right in front of us!"

At the same time, I blasted the horn and tried to grab the siren. But I missed. Right then, I heard a loud, scared wail — just like the siren would make — but it wasn't from me. Jack had reached for the siren too, and our hands bumped into each other.

We drove slowly through the dust cloud. I hadn't put my goggles back on after leaving King's Lynn, and the dust stung my eyes. This wasn't fog — it was real road dust. As we crept forward, I felt Harry's hand grab my shoulder.

"There's something ahead," he said. "Look! Don't you see the tail light?"

But I didn't. We kept rolling forward very slowly, and when we came out of the dust, the road was completely empty. There were hedges on both sides, and no turn-offs anywhere. On the right side, there was a small lodge with gates — but the gates were closed, and the lodge was dark.

We came to a stop. The night air was perfectly still — not a single leaf was moving. No dust rose from the road. But behind us, the dust cloud hung in the air, stopped at the closed gates. We had moved so slowly that it seemed impossible the cloud had come from us.

Then Jack spoke, his voice sounding strange and tight.

"It must have been another car, sir. But where is it?"

I didn't have an answer. Then Harry, speaking from the backseat, said something. His voice was shaky, and for a second, I didn't even recognize it.

"Did you hit the siren?" he asked. "It didn't sound like ours. It sounded like... like something else."

"I didn't touch it," I said.

We drove on. After a while, we saw lights from houses along the road.

"What place is this?" I asked Jack.

"Bircham, sir," he answered.

Gavon's Eve

Only the biggest, most detailed maps even bother to show the tiny village of Gavon in Sutherland. It's surprising that any map would mark it at all—a small, tightly packed group of huts sitting on a cold, empty headland between the moor and the sea. It seems like the kind of place that wouldn't matter to anyone who didn't live there. But the river Gavon, which flows past this handful of battered houses, is well-known to people outside the village. The salmon there are big, the river's mouth is clear of nets, and for six miles upstream, the coffee-colored water forms one deep pool after another. When the river is in good condition and you're even a little hopeful, you're almost guaranteed to catch something.

During the first two weeks of September, I never had a day without a catch on that beautiful river. Every day until the 15th, someone staying at the lodge where I was staying pulled a fish from the famous Picts' Pool. But after the 15th, nobody fished there again. Here's why.

At that spot, the river rushes through about a hundred yards of rapids, then makes a sharp turn around a rocky point and crashes into the pool. The water is deep at the start, but it gets even deeper further down on the east side, where a dark, fast back-current pulls upstream again. You can only fish it from the west bank. On the east side, a huge wall of black rock rises straight up about sixty feet from the river. It's jagged at the top and so thin that there's a hole near the middle of it, like a narrow window, where you can see daylight through the rock. Nobody would want to fish while standing on that sharp, dangerous edge, so everyone fishes from the west side. Thankfully, a good cast covers the whole pool.

On the western bank are the remains of the structure that gave the pool its name—the ruins of an old Pict castle. It's made of rough, unpolished stones stacked without mortar, but it's big and still in good condition, considering how ancient it is. It's round and about twenty yards across. A staircase of large stone blocks leads up to the main gate, and on the side facing the river, there's a smaller gate. A steep, tricky path leads down from there to the riverbank, where you have to be careful and agile to get down safely. There's still a roof over the gate-chamber, and inside the walls you can see the remains of three rooms. In the middle is a very deep hole, probably an old well. Just outside the small river gate is a flat platform, about twenty feet across, which looks like it once held another structure. Some stone slabs are scattered around it.

The nearest post town, Brora, is about six miles southwest. From there, you can follow a track across the moor to the rapids above the Picts' Pool. If the river is low, you can jump from rock to rock and cross the river dry-foot, then climb up a steep path north of the black rock to reach the village. But it's not an easy trip—you need a steady head and good balance. The main road between Gavon and Brora makes a big loop over the moor and passes the gates of Gavon Lodge, where I was staying.

For some unclear reason, both the pool and the old castle had a bad reputation among the local people. Sometimes when I was walking back after a day of fishing, my gillie would take a much longer path home, even when carrying heavy fish, just to avoid passing the castle at dusk. The first time Sandy, my gillie—a tall, strong, yellow-bearded man of about twenty-five—did this, he said the ground around the castle was "too boggy." As a good Christian, he must have known he wasn't telling the truth. Another time, he admitted it more plainly: he said the Picts' Pool wasn't a place to be near after sunset. Now, I'm inclined to agree with him. When he lied, it wasn't out of disrespect—it was because he feared the devil as much as he feared God.

On the evening of September 14, I was walking back with my host, Hugh Graham, after a day in the forest beyond the lodge. It had been unusually hot for September, and the hills were covered with soft, heavy clouds. Sandy followed behind us with the ponies. As we walked, I casually told Hugh about Sandy's strange fear of the Picts' Pool after dark. Hugh frowned a little as he listened.

"That's odd," he said. "I know there's some old superstition about the place, but last year Sandy used to laugh about it. I remember asking him once, and he said the whole thing was nonsense. But this year you say he avoids it?"

"He's avoided it several times with me," I said.

Hugh walked silently for a bit, the heather soft underfoot.

"Poor guy," he said at last. "I'm not sure what to do with him. He's becoming less dependable."

"Is it because of drinking?" I asked.

"Yes, but not exactly. The drinking came second. First came trouble—and now that trouble might be leading him into something worse than drinking."

"The only thing worse than drinking is the devil," I said.

"Exactly. And I think that's where he's headed. He goes there often."

"What do you mean?" I asked.

"Well, it's strange," Hugh said. "You know I've always been interested in folklore and old beliefs. And I think I'm on the trail of something really unusual. Hold on a moment."

We stood still in the thickening dusk, waiting for the ponies. Soon they came up the hill toward us, Sandy walking easily beside them, looking like the long day's work hadn't tired him at all.

"Off to visit Mistress Macpherson again tonight?" Hugh asked him.

"Aye, poor soul," Sandy said. "She's old, and she's all alone."

"Very kind of you, Sandy," Hugh said, and we kept walking.

When the ponies had fallen behind again, I asked, "Well? What's the story?"

"Superstition still lives here," Hugh said. "People believe Mistress Macpherson is a witch. Honestly, the idea fascinates me. If you asked me under oath whether I believe in witches, I'd probably say no. But if you asked me under oath whether I suspect I believe in them, I might have to say yes. And tomorrow, the fifteenth of September, is Gavon's Eve."

"What in the world is Gavon's Eve?" I asked. "And who is Gavon? And what's the trouble?"

"Gavon is probably the old hero this place is named after—not a saint, just an important figure. As for the trouble, it's Sandy's trouble. It's a long story. But we still have a good mile to walk, if you want to hear it."

During that mile, Hugh told me the story. About a year ago, Sandy had gotten engaged to a girl from Gavon who worked in Inverness. In March, without telling anyone, he traveled there to visit her. As he was walking down the street where she lived, he suddenly ran into her. She wasn't alone—she was with a man who spoke with a clipped English accent and acted like a gentleman. The man tipped his hat to Sandy and greeted him warmly, acting as if it was completely normal to be out walking with Catrine. It didn't seem suspicious at the time, especially since Catrine was clearly happy to see Sandy. For the moment, Sandy was satisfied.

But after he returned to Gavon, doubts started to creep into his mind. His suspicions grew, like weeds, and about a month ago he had written a long, messy letter to Catrine, begging her to come home so they could get married right away. People later found out that she had left Inverness and taken the train to Brora. From there, she set out on foot to cross the moor to Gavon, following the path that passed above the Picts' Castle and across the rapids. She left her luggage to be delivered later by a carrier. But she never arrived in Gavon. Some said that even though it was a hot afternoon, she had been wearing a big cloak.

By now we had reached the lodge, its lights looking blurry through the thick mist that had rolled down from the hills.

"And the rest," said Hugh, "which sounds even stranger than this part, I'll tell you later."

In my opinion, deciding to go to bed is as hard as deciding to get up in the morning. Even after our long day, I was secretly glad when Hugh came back to the smoking room, looking lively. It showed that he wasn't ready for bed either, even though the other men had already gone off yawning after their candles.

"So about Sandy—" I started.

"I was thinking the same," Hugh said. "Well, here's where it stands. Catrine Gordon left Brora, but she never made it to Gavon. That's a fact. Now for the stranger part. Do you remember ever seeing a woman walking alone on the moor near the loch? I think I once pointed her out to you."

"Yes, I remember," I said. "Surely not Catrine? She looked ancient—terrible, honestly. She had a mustache, whiskers, and she muttered to herself. Always staring at the ground."

"That's her—not Catrine, of course. That's Mrs. Macpherson, the one people say is a witch. Anyway, Sandy now walks a mile or more every night to visit her. You know what Sandy is like—a tall, strong, handsome man. Now tell me—can you think of any normal reason why he would spend his evenings visiting an old hag in the hills?"

"It sounds unlikely," I admitted.

"Unlikely? That's putting it mildly."

Hugh got up and crossed the room to a bookcase filled with old, dusty books. He pulled down a small leather-bound volume.

"Superstitions of Sutherlandshire," he said, handing it to me. "Turn to page 128 and read."

I flipped to the page and started reading:

"September 15 was believed to be the night of a devil's festival. On this night, the powers of darkness ruled. Anyone out after dark who asked for their help would not be protected by God. Witches were especially powerful on this night. Any witch could make a young man fall in love with her by using a love charm. Even if he was engaged or married, every year on that night, he would belong to her—unless, by some sudden act of grace, he called on God's name. In that case, her magic would fail. Also on this night, witches could use dark spells and terrible curses to raise from the dead those who had committed suicide."

"Top of the next page," said Hugh. "Skip the next paragraph—it's not important for this."

I continued reading:

"Near a small village called Gavon, the moon is said to shine at midnight through a crack in a rock wall beside the river. Its light falls directly onto the ruins of a Pict castle, hitting a large flat stone near the gate. Some believe this stone was once a pagan altar. At that exact moment, the evil spirits who are strongest on Gavon's Eve reach the height of their power. Anyone who dares call on them there can get whatever they wish—but at terrible risk to their soul."

The paragraph ended there, and I closed the book.

"Well?" I asked.

"When things add up properly, two and two make four," said Hugh.

"And four means—what exactly?" I asked.

"This," Hugh said. "Sandy has definitely been meeting with a woman believed to be a witch—someone no local farmer would even dare pass by after dark. He's desperate to find out what happened to Catrine, no matter what it costs him. I think it's very possible that tomorrow night, at midnight, people will gather at the Picts' Pool. There's another strange thing too. I was fishing there yesterday, and right by the river gate of the old castle, I saw that someone had dragged a huge flat stone from the rubble at the bottom of the slope and set it up."

"You mean that old woman might try to bring back Catrine's body—if she's dead?" I asked.

"Yes. And I want to see it with my own eyes. Come with me."

The next day, Hugh and I went fishing along the river, bringing another gillie instead of Sandy. We caught two fish and had lunch sitting on the slope near the Picts' Castle. Just like Hugh said, a large flat stone had been dragged onto the platform outside the river gate. It rested on some rough supports, which now clearly seemed built for it.

The stone was placed exactly across from the narrow window cut through the black rock wall on the other side of the pool. If the moon shone through the window at midnight, its light would fall directly on the stone. It was obvious that this would be the center of whatever ritual was planned.

Below the platform, the ground dropped sharply to the pool's edge. The river was running very high after rain on the hills, and the surface was streaked with bubbles as the water roared by. The sound filled the air and made it hard to hear anything else. But underneath the steep wall of rock across the pool, the water was still, dark, and deep. Above the platform, seven worn stone steps led up to the castle gate, which was framed by the old circular wall rising about four feet high. Inside the castle, the ruins of three chambers could still be seen, divided by broken walls. Hugh and I decided to hide in the chamber closest to the river gate. From there, we could hear any movement and see, through the broken gate, whatever happened at the stone altar or down by the pool.

The lodge was only about a ten-minute walk away if we cut straight across, so we planned to leave around a quarter to twelve. We would sneak in through the gate farthest from the river, making sure no one saw or heard us.

That night, the air was heavy and completely still. Just before midnight, we slipped out of the lodge. The sky in the east was clear, but thick black clouds were creeping up from the west, covering most of the stars. Every now and then, a flash of lightning blinked from the edge of the clouds, and we heard soft rumbles of thunder far away. Even so, the air around us felt heavy and tense, as if a second, closer storm was about to break.

To the east, the sky stayed light, and the edges of the clouds glittered with stars. By the soft gray glow over the moor, it was clear the moon was about to rise. I told myself the strange, tense feeling in my chest was just the stormy air, but I couldn't shake it. My nerves felt raw.

We had both worn rubber-soled shoes to move quietly. As we walked down to the pool, the only sounds were our own muffled footsteps and the distant thunder. We climbed the steps to the gate farthest from the river and carefully moved along the inside wall toward the river gate. When we peered out, at first I could barely see anything. The huge rock wall across the pool cast a deep black shadow. Slowly, my eyes adjusted, and I could make out the glimmering foam streaks on the surface of the river.

The river was even higher and louder than it had been earlier that day. Its roar was deafening. Only at the very bottom of the far rock wall did the water stay still and dark—the deep backwater that never foamed.

Then I spotted movement—a black shape coming toward us out of the darkness. I watched as a woman's head, then shoulders, and finally her whole figure rose against the pale foam. A man followed behind her. They walked up to the stone altar and stood side by side, silhouetted against the churning white water. Hugh tapped my arm to make sure I saw them too. It was clear from his size and shape that the man was Sandy.

Suddenly, a narrow beam of light shot across the darkness. It grew slowly, until a long, thin shaft of moonlight, shining through the cut in the rock wall, hit the riverbank. The light moved until it fell perfectly between the two figures, glowing faintly blue as it lit up the stone altar.

At that moment, a horrible sound broke over the roar of the river—a woman's voice, screaming. Her arms shot up as if she were calling something down from the sky. At first, I couldn't make out any words. But as she shouted the same things again and again, they started to sink into my mind like a nightmare. She was yelling terrible, evil curses—praising Satan by every name she could think of, and cursing everything that was holy.

Then, as suddenly as it had begun, her screaming stopped. For a few seconds, there was only the endless roaring of the river.

Then the awful voice rose again.

"So, Catrine Gordon," it screamed, "I call you, in the name of my master and yours, to rise from where you lie. Get up—get up!"

Again, everything went silent. I heard Hugh next to me gasp and draw a shaky breath. His hand pointed unsteadily toward the black water under the rock. I looked too—and I saw.

Right beneath the rock, a faint, underwater light began to glow and flicker in the moving river. At first, it was tiny and weak. But as we watched, it grew bigger, like it was rising from the deep. Soon it lit up an area about a yard across. Then the surface of the water broke, and a girl's head appeared—white as death, with long hair flowing around her. Her eyes were closed, and her mouth drooped as if she were peacefully asleep. The water curled around her neck like a frill.

Slowly, her body rose higher and higher from the river until she stood visible up to her waist, glowing faintly as if lit from within. Her head was bowed toward her chest, and her hands were clasped tightly together. As she came out of the water, it seemed like she drifted closer, even though the river's current was strong. Now she was halfway across the pool, calmly moving against the rushing flood.

Then, from the darkness, a man's voice cried out in a strangled, desperate tone.

"Catrine! Catrine! In God's name—in God's name!"

In two huge steps, Sandy rushed down the steep riverbank and threw himself into the raging water. I saw his arms fling upward once—and then he disappeared beneath the surface. At the same moment he called Catrine's name, the ghostly figure vanished too. Instantly after, a blinding flash of light exploded in front of us, followed by a crack of thunder so loud and terrible that I hid my face in my hands.

Right away, it was as if the sky itself had torn open. A solid sheet of water came crashing down on us. It wasn't like rain—it was like standing under a waterfall. We crouched there, soaked to the skin, as the storm poured over us.

Any thought of saving Sandy was hopeless. Jumping into that wild river would mean instant death, and even if someone could survive the current, there was no way to find him in the total darkness. Besides, even if it had been possible, I'm not sure I could have forced myself to dive into the same water where that ghost had risen.

As we crouched there, another fear gripped me—the woman. She had been somewhere close by, screaming those horrible words that had made my blood turn cold. I couldn't stand it any longer.

"I can't stay here," I said to Hugh. "I have to run—right now. Where is she?"

"Didn't you see?" he asked.

"No. What happened?" I said.

"The lightning hit the stone—just inches from where she was standing. We... we have to go look for her."

I followed him down the slope, shaking so badly it felt like I had no control over my body. I stumbled forward with my hands out in front of me, terrified I might touch something—or someone.

The storm clouds had now covered the moon completely. No light from the crack in the rock helped guide us. In the darkness, we searched along the bank—from the shattered stone down to the edge of the pool. But we found nothing.

Finally, we gave up. It seemed certain that the woman had been struck by the lightning and had fallen down the bank into the water—disappearing into the same dark pool where she had tried to summon the dead.

Nobody fished at the Picts' Pool the next day. Instead, men came from Brora with drag nets. They found two bodies lying together in the deep backwater under the rock: Sandy and the dead girl. But of the woman, they found no trace.

It seems that when Catrine Gordon got Sandy's letter, she left Inverness, deeply troubled. What happened next is only a guess. Maybe she tried to take the shortcut across the river by stepping on the rocks above the Picts' Pool—and slipped. Or maybe, unable to face her future, she jumped in on purpose. We'll never know for sure.

Either way, they now rest side by side in the cold, windy graveyard at Brora, following the mysterious will of God.

The Confession of Charles Linkworth

Dr. Teesdale had to visit the condemned man a few times during the week before his execution. He found him calm and accepting of his fate, which is often the case once a prisoner realizes there's no hope left. Charles Linkworth didn't seem afraid of the morning that kept creeping closer hour by hour. It was as if the hardest part—accepting he would die—was already behind him the moment he learned his appeal had been denied. But during the days when he still had a little hope, he had suffered terribly, facing death every single day in his mind.

In all his years of work, the doctor had never seen anyone cling to life so desperately or be so deeply tied to the physical world by a sheer, animal-like urge to keep living. But once hope was gone, Linkworth let go. It was such a sudden change that Dr. Teesdale wondered if he was truly at peace, or if the shock had simply numbed him, leaving him alive inside but too stunned to show it.

Linkworth had fainted when he first heard the final decision, and Dr. Teesdale was called to treat him. But the fainting spell was brief, and he quickly came back to full awareness, fully understanding what had happened.

The murder itself had been especially awful, and the public had no sympathy for him. Charles Linkworth had run a small stationery shop in Sheffield. He lived there with his wife and his mother—the same mother he murdered. His motive was simple: he wanted to steal the five hundred pounds that belonged to her.

At the time, Linkworth was about a hundred pounds in debt. While his wife was away visiting family, he strangled his mother and, during the night, buried her body in the small backyard garden. When his wife returned, he had a believable story ready. For years, he and his mother had argued a lot, and she had often threatened to leave and take her small weekly contribution of eight shillings with her. She had even talked about using her money to buy an annuity and live somewhere else.

It was also true that during his wife's absence, he and his mother had another nasty argument—this one over something small—and she had pulled her money out of the bank, planning to leave for London the next day to live near friends. That evening, she told him her plans. That night, he killed her.

Afterward, he acted with cold logic. Before his wife came home, he packed up all of his mother's belongings and sent them by passenger train to London. That evening, he invited friends over for supper and told them his mother had left. He didn't pretend to be sad about it—he said he and his mother had never gotten along and that her leaving had brought peace to the house.

When his wife returned, he told her the same story, adding that the final argument had been so bad his mother hadn't even left an address. This detail was clever—it stopped his wife from trying to contact her. She believed him completely. Nothing about his story seemed strange.

For a while, Linkworth behaved with the same careful planning that many criminals show—until eventually they make a mistake. He didn't immediately spend the money. Instead, he rented out his mother's room to a young man and fired his shop assistant, taking over all the work himself. This gave the impression he was cutting costs. He even talked openly about how well the shop was now doing.

It wasn't until a month later that he finally used some of the stolen money. He exchanged two fifty-pound notes and paid off his debts.

But after that, his careful behavior began to fall apart. Instead of slowly adding to his savings like a cautious man would, he opened a new deposit account at a local bank with four more fifty-pound notes.

He also became nervous about the body buried in the garden. Thinking it would be safer if he hid it better, he had a cartload of rocks and broken stone delivered. In the evenings, after work, he and his lodger built a fake rock garden over the grave.

Then a random accident set everything in motion. There was a fire in the lost luggage office at King's Cross Station, where his mother's boxes were still sitting. One of the boxes was partially burned. Since the railway company was responsible for lost luggage, they looked inside for identification. They found her name on some clothing and a letter with the Sheffield address. This led to an official notice being sent to Mrs. Linkworth, offering compensation.

The letter arrived at the house—and it was Linkworth's wife who read it.

It seemed harmless enough. But for Charles Linkworth, it was the beginning of the end. He couldn't explain why his mother's belongings were still at King's Cross. His only excuse was that something must have happened to her. But clearly, if there was an accident, they needed to go to the police to find her—and, if necessary, to claim her property. His wife and his lodger, who were both present when the letter was read aloud, insisted he take action. He couldn't refuse without making them suspicious.

After that, the silent, steady machinery of justice went to work. Men quietly watched his house, observed the supposed boom in his shop, checked the local banks, and kept an eye on the backyard, where ferns were already growing over the fake rock garden.

Soon after came his arrest and the trial, which didn't take long. On a certain Saturday night, the jury reached its verdict.

The courtroom was packed. Smartly dressed women in large hats brought bright colors to the scene, but no one there had any sympathy for the athletic-looking young man being sentenced. Many of the onlookers were respectable mothers themselves, and they were outraged by his crime against his own mother. They listened carefully, approving every piece of flawless evidence against him.

They watched, almost thrilled, as the judge put on the small black cap and spoke the final, grim sentence that, by law and by tradition, had to be said.

Linkworth went to his execution with the same calm indifference he had shown ever since he learned his appeal had been denied. No one who heard the evidence could doubt he was guilty. The prison chaplain had done everything he could to get Linkworth to confess, but it had no effect. Until the end, Linkworth quietly insisted he was innocent, though he didn't protest much.

On a bright September morning, with the sun shining warmly over the grim little group crossing the prison yard toward the place where the gallows stood, justice was carried out. Dr. Teesdale was there, and he was sure death was immediate. He had watched everything: the bolt being pulled, the hooded figure dropping, and the rope creaking under the sudden weight. He had seen the quick, jerky movements of the hanging body, which lasted only a second or two. The execution was completely successful.

An hour later, Dr. Teesdale performed the post-mortem examination. It confirmed what he already believed—the vertebrae at the neck had been snapped clean, meaning death had been instant.

Even though there was no real need, he made the small cut that officially proved it, just to be thorough.

At that moment, he had a strange, vivid feeling that Linkworth's spirit was still nearby, lingering close to his broken body. Yet there was no doubt the body was dead—it had been for an hour.

Then something odd happened. A prison guard came in and asked if the rope used in the execution—normally kept as the hangman's reward—had accidentally been brought into the mortuary. But the rope had completely vanished. It wasn't there, it wasn't still on the scaffold, and no one could explain what had happened to it. Although it wasn't a big problem, the disappearance was certainly strange.

Dr. Teesdale was a bachelor with his own money. He lived in a large house with tall windows in Bedford Square. A brilliant cook prepared his meals, and her husband handled other household needs. He didn't have to work, but chose to serve as a prison doctor because he was fascinated by the minds of criminals.

He believed most crimes—the breaking of society's rules for survival—came either from brain problems or from poverty. Theft, for example, was sometimes because of real hunger, but just as often because of a hidden mental disorder. In extreme cases, it was called kleptomania, but he thought there were many unrecognized cases, too. This was especially true when violence was part of the crime.

As he went home that night, he thought about Linkworth. The crime had been terrible, and the need for money wasn't desperate enough to explain such horror. In his mind, Linkworth seemed more like someone insane than a typical criminal. Before the murder, he had been known as a good man—kind, a loyal husband, and a friendly neighbor. Then, suddenly, he committed one monstrous act that put him completely outside human society.

Whether sane or insane, a person who could do such a thing had no place in the world. Still, Dr. Teesdale felt uneasy. It bothered him that Linkworth had never confessed. Even though there was no real doubt about his guilt, it would have felt better if Linkworth had admitted it himself when there was nothing left to lose.

That evening, Dr. Teesdale ate dinner alone. Afterward, he sat in the study next to the dining room. Feeling too restless to read, he settled into his large red chair by the fireplace and let his thoughts wander. Almost immediately, he found himself thinking again about the strange sensation he had had earlier—that Linkworth's spirit had still been there in the mortuary.

It wasn't the first time he had felt something like that, especially after sudden deaths. But today the feeling had been stronger, clearer than ever before. To him, it didn't seem unreasonable. He believed in life after death and thought the soul didn't vanish instantly when the body died. Instead, it might hang around for a while, still tied to the earth.

In his spare time, Dr. Teesdale had studied the occult. Like many experienced doctors, he understood how thin the line was between the mind and the body, between the seen and the unseen. It made sense to him that a spirit might still be able to communicate with the living.

His thoughts were starting to form a clear pattern when he was interrupted. His telephone sat nearby on his desk. It rang—but not with its usual sharp, metallic sound. Instead, it was faint and weak, like the electricity wasn't strong enough or the machine was damaged. Still, it was ringing.

He got up, lifted the receiver, and spoke into it.

"Yes, yes," he said. "Who is it?"

There was a whisper on the other end of the line—so quiet it was almost impossible to hear, and he couldn't make out the words.

"I can't hear you," he said.

The whisper came again, just as faint and unclear. Then it stopped altogether.

He stood there for about half a minute, waiting to see if the voice would return. All he heard was the usual crackling and clicking noises that showed the phone was still connected to another line. After a moment, he hung up the receiver, called the telephone exchange, and gave them his number.

"Can you tell me which number just called me?" he asked.

After a short wait, they told him. It was the number for the prison where he worked.

"Connect me, please," he said.

Once the connection was made, he spoke into the receiver. "You called me just now," he said. "I'm Dr. Teesdale. What was it? I couldn't hear you clearly."

The voice on the other end came back, clear and easy to understand.

"There's been a mistake, sir," it said. "We didn't call you."

"But the exchange told me it was your number, three minutes ago."

"Must've been a mistake at the exchange, sir," the voice answered.

"Very strange. Well, good night. Is this Warder Draycott?"

"Yes, sir. Good night, sir."

Dr. Teesdale went back to his large armchair, even less interested in reading now. He sat there for a while, letting his thoughts drift. But no matter where his mind wandered, it kept returning to the odd incident with the telephone.

He had been called by mistake before, and sometimes he'd been connected to the wrong number. But there was something different about this—something about the weak, almost ghostly ringing and the faint whisper that suggested something stranger. Soon he found himself pacing up and down the room, thinking deeply about it.

"But it's impossible," he said aloud.

The next morning, he went to the prison as usual. Right away, he felt it again—that strong sense that something unseen was around him. He had experienced strange things before and knew he was what people call "sensitive"—someone who could, under certain conditions, sense things from the unseen world.

That morning, he clearly felt the presence of the man who had been executed the day before. It felt strongest in the small prison yard and near the door of the condemned cell. The feeling was so intense that he half-expected to see Linkworth's figure appear in front of him. When he walked through the door at the end of the passage, he even turned around, certain he might see something.

All the while, he felt a deep, growing horror inside him. This unseen presence disturbed him terribly. He felt sure the poor spirit wanted something—but what, he didn't know. Dr. Teesdale was convinced it wasn't just his imagination. The spirit of Charles Linkworth was truly there.

He moved on to the infirmary and worked for a couple of hours, but even there, he could sense the ghost nearby—though not as strongly as near the cell or the yard. Before leaving, he decided to test his feelings. He went into the execution shed.

The moment he stepped inside, his face went pale, and he hurriedly backed out, slamming the door behind him.

At the top of the steps inside, he had seen something—hazy and faint, but real: the hooded and tied-up figure of a man. It was blurry, like a misty shadow, but he had no doubt it was there.

Dr. Teesdale had strong nerves, and he quickly recovered from the shock, embarrassed by his brief panic. The fear that had drained the color from his face had more to do with startled nerves than true terror. Still, although he was deeply fascinated by the supernatural, he couldn't force himself to go back inside.

Or rather, he tried—but his body refused to move. If the ghost wanted to communicate, he would much rather it happen from a distance. It seemed that the spirit could only reach places tied closely to its death: the prison yard, the condemned cell, the execution shed—and, less strongly, the infirmary.

Then another thought struck him. He returned to his office and sent for Warder Draycott, the man he had spoken to on the telephone the night before.

"You're completely sure," Dr. Teesdale asked, "that nobody used the phone to call me just before I rang you?"

Draycott hesitated, and the doctor immediately noticed.

"I don't see how it's possible, sir," he said. "I was sitting right by the telephone for half an hour before that—and before that, too. I would have seen anyone who used it."

"And you didn't see anyone?" Dr. Teesdale asked, putting slight pressure on the word.

Draycott looked even more uncomfortable.

"No, sir, I saw no one," he repeated carefully.

The doctor looked away, pretending not to notice his unease.

"But maybe you felt like someone was there?" he asked casually, as if it didn't matter much.

It was clear Draycott was struggling with something he didn't want to say.

"Well, sir, if you put it that way," he said slowly, "maybe. But you'll just say I was half-asleep, or that I ate something bad at supper."

Dr. Teesdale dropped the casual tone.

"I would never say that," he said. "Just like I wouldn't say I was dreaming last night when I heard my telephone ring. It didn't sound normal, Draycott. It was so faint I could barely hear it, even though I was right next to it. And when I answered, all I could hear was a whisper. But when you spoke, I heard you clearly.

"I believe something—or someone—was at my end of the telephone. And you were there, too. You didn't see anything—but you felt something."

The man nodded.

"I'm not the kind of man who gets scared easily, sir," said Draycott. "And I don't imagine things. But there was definitely something there. It stayed near the telephone, and it wasn't the wind—there wasn't even a breeze, and the night was warm. I even shut the window to be sure. But whatever it was moved around the room for over an hour. It rustled the pages of the telephone book, and when it got close to me, it brushed my hair. And it was ice cold, sir."

The doctor stared straight at him.

"Did it remind you of what happened yesterday morning?" he asked quickly.

Draycott hesitated for a moment, then answered.

"Yes, sir. It made me think of Convict Charles Linkworth."

Dr. Teesdale gave him a calm nod.

"That's what I thought," he said. "Now, are you on duty again tonight?"

"Yes, sir. Though I wish I wasn't."

"I know exactly how you feel. I've felt the same way. Whatever this thing is, it seems to want to talk to me. By the way, did anything unusual happen in the prison last night?"

"Yes, sir. About half a dozen men had terrible nightmares. They were yelling and screaming—quiet men, usually. It's not the first time men have bad dreams after an execution, but I've never seen it as bad as last night."

"I understand. Now listen carefully. If whatever it is tries to use the telephone again tonight, let it. Don't interrupt unless you absolutely have to. It will probably happen around the same time as yesterday. That's usually how these things work. So, between nine-thirty and ten-thirty, stay away from the room with the phone. Give it plenty of time. I'll be waiting on my end. And after it's over, I'll call you back just to make sure it wasn't a regular call."

"And there's really nothing to be afraid of, sir?" Draycott asked.

Dr. Teesdale remembered his own fear that morning but answered honestly.

"I'm sure there's nothing to be afraid of," he said.

That evening, Dr. Teesdale canceled his dinner plans and stayed in his study by nine-thirty. He knew that no one fully understood why spirits, if they existed, seemed to appear at certain hours over and over. But from what he had learned, especially in cases where a spirit was desperate for help, they often came at the same time each day.

Usually, a spirit's ability to show itself grew stronger shortly after death, then slowly weakened as time passed.

Tonight, he expected the spirit to be even stronger.

Right around the same time as before, the telephone rang. It wasn't quite as faint as the night before, but it still wasn't the usual loud ring.

Dr. Teesdale quickly stood up and picked up the receiver.

The sound he heard made his blood run cold—deep, heart-wrenching sobs, as if someone was crying from the bottom of their soul.

He waited a moment, his heart pounding with fear, but also with a strong desire to help.

"Yes, yes," he finally said, hearing his own voice tremble. "This is Dr. Teesdale. What can I do for you? Who are you?" he added, although deep down, he already knew.

The sobbing slowly faded into broken whispers.

"I want to tell... sir—I need to tell—I must tell," the voice said.

"Yes, tell me. What is it?" the doctor asked.

"No, not you... another gentleman who used to visit me. Will you pass on what I say? I can't make him hear me or see me."

"Who are you?" Dr. Teesdale asked quickly.

"Charles Linkworth. I thought you knew. I'm very miserable. I can't leave the prison—and it's so cold. Will you bring the other gentleman?"

"Do you mean the chaplain?" asked Dr. Teesdale.

"Yes, the chaplain. He read the service for me when I crossed the yard yesterday. I won't feel so miserable once I tell."

The doctor paused, thinking it over. It would be strange to tell Mr. Dawkins, the chaplain, that Charles Linkworth's spirit was on the other end of the telephone. But Dr. Teesdale believed it was true. He believed the poor man's soul was trapped, desperate to confess.

There was no need to ask what Linkworth wanted to confess. He already knew.

"Yes," Dr. Teesdale said at last. "I'll ask him to come here."

"Thank you, sir, a thousand times. You'll bring him, won't you?"

The voice was fading fast.

"It has to be tomorrow night," it said. "I can't stay any longer. I have to go see—oh, my God, my God..."

The sobbing started again, growing weaker and weaker. Dr. Teesdale leaned closer, desperate to hear more.

"See what?" he cried. "Tell me what's happening! What are you doing?"

"I can't tell you... I'm not allowed," whispered the voice. "That's part of it—"

Then it disappeared completely.

Dr. Teesdale stood still, listening. All he could hear now was the soft crackling of the telephone line. He slowly hung up the receiver, only then realizing that his forehead was wet with cold sweat. His heart was racing, and his ears buzzed. He sat down heavily, trying to pull himself together.

He briefly wondered if someone was playing a cruel joke on him—but he knew deep down it wasn't. He was certain he had spoken to a soul in deep misery, trapped by guilt over a terrible crime. There was no doubt in his mind: in his safe, comfortable home, with the sounds of London in the background, he had spoken with the spirit of Charles Linkworth.

But there was no time to dwell on it. His nerves were still shaken. He quickly picked up the phone and called the prison.

"Warder Draycott?" he asked when the line connected.

The man's voice shook slightly when he answered.

"Yes, sir. Is that you, Dr. Teesdale?"

"Yes. Has anything unusual happened there?"

The man tried twice to answer but couldn't. On the third try, he managed to speak.

"Yes, sir. He was here. I saw him go into the room with the telephone."

"Did you speak to him?"

"No, sir. I just sat and prayed. And half a dozen of the men were screaming in their sleep again. But it's quiet now. I think... I think he's gone to the execution shed."

"All right. I don't think there will be any more trouble tonight. By the way, can you give me Mr. Dawkins' home address?"

The warder gave it to him, and Dr. Teesdale sat down to write a letter to the chaplain. But when he tried to write at his desk—right next to the telephone—he found he couldn't. His nerves were still too raw.

Instead, he went upstairs to the drawing-room, a space he only used when guests visited. There, feeling calmer, he wrote a note asking Mr. Dawkins to have dinner with him the next night. He said he had something very strange to share and needed his help.

"Even if you already have plans," he wrote, "please cancel them. I did the same tonight, and I would have regretted it if I hadn't."

The next evening, they had dinner together. After the meal, when they were left alone with coffee and cigarettes, Dr. Teesdale began.

"You must promise not to think I'm crazy, Dawkins," he said. "Promise before I tell you."

Mr. Dawkins laughed lightly.

"I promise. I won't think you're crazy," he said.

"Good. Because last night—and the night before—I spoke through the telephone with the spirit of Charles Linkworth, the man we saw executed two days ago."

This time, the chaplain didn't laugh. He pushed back his chair, frowning.

"Teesdale," he said sharply, "is this why you asked me here tonight? To tell me a ghost story?"

"Yes. And you haven't even heard the most important part. Last night, Linkworth asked me to find you. He wants to tell you something. And I think we both know what it is."

Dawkins stood up.

"I don't want to hear any more," he said firmly. "The dead don't come back. What happens after death isn't for us to know. But they have nothing more to do with this world."

"But you need to hear this," insisted the doctor. "Two nights ago, I got a call—so faint I could only hear whispers. I checked with the exchange right away, and they said it came from the prison. I called the prison, and Draycott said no one had touched the phone. He also felt a presence."

"I think that man drinks," Dawkins said sharply.

The doctor looked at him calmly.

"My dear fellow, you shouldn't say that. Draycott is one of the most trustworthy men we have. And if you think he's drunk, you might as well accuse me too."

The chaplain sat down again.

"Forgive me," he said. "But I don't want to get involved in this. It's dangerous to mess with things like that. And how do you know it's not just a trick?"

"Played by who?" asked the doctor. He paused, listening. "Wait—listen!"

The telephone bell suddenly rang again. It was a clear, undeniable sound to Dr. Teesdale.

"Don't you hear it?" he asked.

"Hear what?" said Dawkins.

"The telephone—it's ringing!"

"I hear nothing," Dawkins said, sounding irritated. "There's no bell ringing."

Dr. Teesdale didn't argue. He walked into the study, turned on the lights, and picked up the phone.

"Yes?" he said, his voice shaking slightly. "Who is it? Yes—Mr. Dawkins is here. I'll try to get him to speak with you."

He rushed back to the dining room.

"Dawkins," he said urgently, "there's a soul in agony. I'm begging you—for God's sake—come and listen."

The chaplain hesitated, then nodded.

"As you wish," he said.

He went into the study, picked up the receiver, and held it to his ear.

"I'm Mr. Dawkins," he said.

He stood there quietly, listening.

"I hear nothing at all," he said after a moment. "Wait—there was something. The faintest whisper."

"Try harder to hear! Please try!" said the doctor.

The chaplain listened again. After a few moments, he set the receiver down with a frown.

"Something—someone said, 'I killed her, I confess it. I want forgiveness.'" He shook his head. "This is a hoax, Teesdale. Someone must know about your interest in spirits and is playing a cruel joke. I can't believe it's real."

Dr. Teesdale picked up the receiver again.

"I'm Dr. Teesdale," he said. "Can you give Mr. Dawkins a sign to prove it's really you?"

Then he set the phone back down.

"He says he thinks he can," Dr. Teesdale explained. "We'll have to wait."

The night was warm, and the window facing the paved yard behind the house was open. For about five minutes, the two men stood silently, waiting. Nothing happened.

"I think that's proof enough," said the chaplain, breaking the silence.

But just as he spoke, a cold gust of air rushed into the room, making the papers on the desk flutter. Dr. Teesdale quickly went to the window and closed it.

"Did you feel that?" he asked.

"Yes, just a sudden chill," the chaplain answered.

Even with the window shut, the air in the room stirred again, even colder this time.

"And did you feel that too?" the doctor asked.

The chaplain nodded, feeling his heart suddenly pounding hard in his chest.

"Defend us from all dangers of this night," he prayed aloud.

"Something's coming," said the doctor.

As he spoke, it happened. In the middle of the room, less than three yards away, a man appeared. His head drooped sideways onto his shoulder, hiding his face. Slowly, he lifted his head with both hands like it was too heavy to move. When he finally faced them, his eyes and tongue were bulging out, and a dark bruise circled his neck.

Then came a sharp thud on the floorboards—and the figure vanished.

But lying on the floor was something new: a piece of rope.

For a long time, neither man spoke. Sweat streamed down the doctor's face, while the chaplain, pale and shaking, whispered prayers.

Finally, with great effort, Dr. Teesdale pulled himself together. He pointed at the rope.

"That rope has been missing since the execution," he said.

Just then, the telephone rang again. This time, the chaplain didn't hesitate. He went straight to it, and the ringing stopped as soon as he picked up the receiver.

He listened for a while without speaking.

"Charles Linkworth," he said at last, "in the presence of God, are you truly sorry for your sin?"

There was a reply too faint for Dr. Teesdale to hear. The chaplain closed his eyes and began to speak. And Dr. Teesdale, moved by what was happening, dropped to his knees as he heard the words of forgiveness.

When the prayer ended, there was silence again.

"I can't hear anything more," said the chaplain, placing the receiver back onto its hook.

A few minutes later, the doctor's man-servant came into the room carrying a tray with drinks. Dr. Teesdale pointed, without turning to look, at the spot where the ghost had appeared.

"Take that rope and burn it, Parker," he said.

There was a pause.

"There's no rope there, sir," said Parker.

At Abdul Ali's Grave

Luxor, as most visitors agree, is a place full of charm. It offers many attractions for travelers—an excellent hotel with a billiard room, a beautiful garden, lots of visitors, a weekly dance on a tourist steamer, quail hunting, a dreamy climate, and incredibly ancient monuments for those interested in history.

But for a small, dedicated group of people, Luxor's true magic doesn't come alive until all of that fades away—when the tourists are gone, the hotel is nearly empty, and even the billiard marker has left for Cairo. When the quail are gone and the heat of the Theban plain is so intense that no one would dare cross it during the day, not even for an audience with Queen Hatshepsut herself, that's when the true spirit of Luxor awakens for them.

Since I respected these people and their opinions, I decided to see for myself. Two years ago, in early June, I stayed behind when most travelers had already left. It didn't take long for me to become a true believer too.

Weston—one of the first among those who understood this hidden charm—and I spent long, lazy days talking about what made summer in Luxor so special. Even though there was some secret ingredient we couldn't fully explain, we could still list a few things that added to its magic:

- Waking up before dawn, feeling no desire to stay in bed.
- Quietly crossing the Nile with our horses in the still, sweet-smelling air of morning.
- That split second before sunrise, when the grey river suddenly

flashes into a sheet of greenish bronze.

- The pink glow that races across the sky from east to west, quickly followed by sunlight lighting up the peaks of the western hills and pouring down like a flood of golden light.
- The soft stirrings of life—the breeze picking up, a lark singing overhead, the boatman calling "Yallah, yallah," and the horses tossing their heads.
- The peaceful ride that followed.
- The wonderful breakfast afterward.
- The long stretch of having nothing to do all day.
- Riding into the desert at sunset, surrounded by the unique, empty scent of warm sand.
- The brilliance of the tropical night.
- Drinking camel's milk.
- Talking with the local fellahin, who are the most charming and unpredictable people—except when tourists are around, when they only seem to care about getting tips.
- And finally, what mattered most for this story: the chance for strange experiences.

The events that led to this story began four days earlier when Abdul Ali, the oldest man in the village, died suddenly. He was said to be rich and very old. His family claimed he had one hundred years of life and one hundred English pounds saved up—one pound for every year. The neatness of these numbers made people believe it had to be true, and within a day of his death, it became accepted fact.

However, there was a big problem. None of those pounds—or even paper money—could be found. Outside the tourist season, cash in Luxor was seen as more magical than real, but now even that magic was missing. Abdul Ali's century of years—and his century of pounds—seemed to have died with him.

Mohamed, his son, who had already been acting like the heir before Abdul died, showed more anger and distress than true mourning.

The truth was, Abdul Ali hadn't been much of a model citizen. Despite his long life and wealth, he had a bad reputation. He drank wine whenever he could, ate during Ramadan without shame, was believed to have the evil eye, and was attended in his final hours by Achmet—a man well known for practicing Black Magic and suspected of an even worse crime: stealing from the newly dead.

In Egypt, digging treasures out of ancient tombs was considered a proud achievement for archaeologists. But robbing the body of a recently dead neighbor was seen as the lowest crime.

Mohamed, who quickly went from tossing dust in the air to nervously biting his nails, told us privately that he believed Achmet had found out where his father's money was hidden. But at the moment of Abdul's death, when he had tried to say something important, Achmet had acted as clueless as everyone else.

Those who knew Achmet's character thought it was more likely that he had almost learned the secret—but missed it just in time.

After Abdul died and was buried, we all went to the funeral feast, where we ended up eating far more roast meat than anyone really wanted—especially at five o'clock on a hot June afternoon. Because we were still full, Weston and I decided to skip dinner later. After our usual evening ride into the desert, we stayed at home and talked with Mohamed, Abdul's son, and Hussein, Abdul's youngest grandson, who was about twenty years old and worked for us as our valet, cook, and housemaid.

They both sat with us and sadly talked about the missing money that Abdul had supposedly left behind. They also shared some shocking stories about Achmet, who had a suspicious habit of hanging around graveyards. They drank coffee and smoked with us—since we had been guests at their father's funeral earlier that day, we treated them more like friends than servants.

After they left, a boy named Machmout came to see us.

Machmout, who says he thinks he's about twelve but isn't really sure, works for us as kitchen helper, groom, and gardener. He also has a strange ability—something like seeing visions, similar to clairvoyance. Weston, who is a member of the Society for Psychical Research (and who once sadly caught a fake medium named Mrs. Blunt), says it's just thought-reading. He's even been keeping notes on some of Machmout's strange performances, thinking they might be important later.

But to me, thought-reading doesn't explain everything that happened after Abdul's funeral. I believe it was either White Magic—a broad name for anything strange—or just Pure Coincidence, which can explain just about anything if you stretch it far enough.

Machmout's way of working this so-called White Magic is simple. He uses something called an "ink-mirror." Normally, he would pour a little black ink into his palm to gaze into it. But since we didn't have much ink lately (the last post-boat from Cairo carrying our supplies got stuck on a sandbank), we found that a small piece of black American cloth, about the size of a coin, worked just as well.

Machmout would stare into the ink or cloth for five to ten minutes. As he stared, the sharp, lively look would leave his face. His wide-open eyes stayed completely fixed on the cloth, and his body would become stiff and frozen, like a statue. Then, without moving even slightly, he would begin describing strange things he saw. He would stay completely still until we wiped away the ink or took the cloth away. Then he would look up and say "Khalás," which means, "It's finished."

We had only hired Machmout about two weeks before, but on his very first night working for us, after he finished his chores, he came upstairs and said, "I will show you White Magic. Give me ink."

That night, he described the front hallway of our house in London. He said there were two horses standing at the door, and that a man and a woman came outside, fed the horses some bread, and then rode away. It sounded so believable that I wrote to my mother the next day, asking her to write down exactly what she had been doing at half-past five (London time) on June 12.

At the exact same time in Egypt, Machmout had also described seeing a lady having tea in a room, which he described in great detail. I'm still waiting for my mother's reply to see if what he saw was accurate.

Weston's explanation for all of this is that pictures of the people and places I know are somehow hidden deep in my mind—even if I'm not aware of them—and that while in a trance, Machmout somehow picks up on these hidden thoughts. He calls it the "subliminal self."

But I have a simpler view: I think there's just no explanation. After all, no thought inside my head could make my brother go outside and ride a horse at the exact time Machmout said he did—unless, of course, Machmout's visions turn out to match perfectly.

Because of that, I prefer to keep an open mind and am ready to believe almost anything. Since Machmout's last strange performance, Weston has been much less eager to convince me to join the Society for Psychical Research. He doesn't sound nearly as calm and scientific about it now.

Machmout refuses to use his powers if other Egyptians are nearby. He says that if someone who knows Black Magic is in the room while he's practicing White Magic, that person could summon a dark spirit to destroy the good spirit helping him. According to Machmout, Black Magic is stronger, and the two forces are enemies.

He says the spirit of White Magic has helped him before in ways that even I find hard to believe, so he's very careful to protect it. He says he's safe with us because Englishmen, like Weston and me, don't know Black Magic.

Once, Machmout said he saw the spirit of Black Magic "between heaven and earth, and between night and day" on the Karnak road. He described the spirit as having skin lighter than most people's, two long teeth sticking out from the corners of his mouth, and huge eyes, white all over, as big as a horse's.

Machmout settled himself comfortably in the corner, and I handed him the piece of black cloth. It usually took a few minutes for him to enter the hypnotic state where he started seeing visions, so I went out to the balcony to cool off. It was the hottest night we'd had so far—three hours after sunset, and the thermometer still showed almost 100 degrees.

The sky above wasn't its usual deep blue but looked grey and hazy, and a gusty, uneasy wind from the south hinted that the dreaded three-day sandstorm, the khamseen, was coming.

A little way up the street was a small café. Outside, Arabs were sitting in the dark, their water pipes glowing and fading like tiny fireflies. Inside, I could hear the sharp click of brass castanets, clashing along with the whiny music from pipes and strings, as a dancing girl performed for the guests—an entertainment loved by the locals but often unpleasant to Europeans.

Looking east, the sky was lighter. The moon was about to rise. As I watched, the huge red disk of the moon cut across the desert's edge, and right then, fittingly, one of the Arabs at the café began chanting in a deep, musical voice:

"I cannot sleep for longing for thee, O full moon.

Far is thy throne over Mecca, slip down, O beloved, to me."

Just after that, I heard the thin, high sound of Machmout's voice beginning to speak, so I went back inside.

We had learned that our experiments worked best if we touched him while he was in this trance. Weston, who was writing at a table by the window, looked up when I entered.

"Take his hand," Weston said. "Right now he's rambling and not making much sense."

"Do you have an explanation for that?" I asked.

"It's similar to talking in your sleep," Weston answered. "Myers says so. Machmout keeps mentioning a tomb. Maybe Abdul's funeral made him think of it. Try suggesting something to him. He responds faster to you than to me."

But a sudden thought crossed my mind.

"Wait," I said. "I want to listen first."

Machmout's head was tilted back a little, and he was holding the piece of cloth above his face. As usual, he spoke very slowly and in a sharp, jerky voice, totally unlike his normal tone.

"There is a tamarisk tree on one side of the grave," he said. "Green beetles are dancing around it. On the other side is a mud wall. There are many graves around, but they are asleep. Only this one is awake—it is moist and not sandy."

"I thought so," Weston said. "He's describing Abdul's grave."

"The red moon sits low on the desert," Machmout went on. "The khamseen is blowing, and dust is everywhere. The moon is red because of the dust, and because it is still low in the sky."

"He's still picking up on real conditions around him," Weston said. "That's interesting. Pinch him to test if he notices."

I pinched Machmout, but he didn't react at all.

"In the last house on the street, there's a man standing in the doorway," Machmout continued in his strange voice. Suddenly, he cried out, "Ah! He knows Black Magic! Don't let him come here! He's leaving the house—no, he's heading toward the moon and the grave! He has Black Magic with him. He carries a knife—and a spade! I can't see his face because the Black Magic hides it from my eyes!"

Weston and I were both frozen, hanging on every word.

"We should go there," Weston said. "This is a chance to test it for real. Listen—"

"He's walking, walking, walking," piped Machmout. "Still going toward the moon and the grave. The moon isn't sitting on the desert anymore—it's risen a little."

I pointed out the window.

"At least that's true," I said.

Weston quickly pulled the cloth from Machmout's hand, and the boy fell silent. A second later, he stretched, rubbed his eyes, and said, "Khalás"—"It's finished."

"Yes, it's finished," I told him.

"Did I tell you about the lady in England?" he asked.

"Yes, you did. Thank you, little Machmout. The White Magic worked very well tonight. Now off to bed."

Machmout nodded and trotted out of the room. Weston closed the door behind him.

"We must hurry," he said. "It's worth going to check this out, even though I wish it wasn't something so frightening. Odd, though—Machmout wasn't even at the funeral, yet he described the grave exactly. What do you think?"

"I think White Magic showed Machmout that someone using Black Magic is heading to Abdul's grave—maybe to rob it," I said firmly.

"And what are we supposed to do when we get there?" Weston asked.

"See the Black Magic at work," I said. "Personally, I'm scared stiff. And so are you."

"There's no such thing as Black Magic," Weston said. "Wait—I have an idea. Give me that orange."

He quickly peeled the orange and cut out two circles from the skin, each about the size of a large coin, plus two long, thin strips. He stuck the circles in his eyes and the strips at the corners of his mouth.

"The spirit of Black Magic?" I asked.

"Exactly," Weston said, wrapping himself in a long black cloak. Even in the bright lamp light, he looked terrifying.

"I don't believe in Black Magic," he said, "but some people do. If we need to scare someone off, we'll use his own fear against him. Now, who do you think it is? I mean—who were you thinking about when your thoughts probably reached Machmout?"

"What Machmout said made me think of Achmet," I replied.

Weston gave a skeptical laugh, and we headed out.

The moon had just lifted off the horizon, just as Machmout had described. At first it glowed deep red, like a faraway fire, but as it rose higher, the color faded into a dull yellow.

The hot south wind, blowing harder and harder, was thick with sand. It hit our faces like a furnace. Palm trees in the abandoned hotel garden thrashed back and forth, making a rattling sound with their dry leaves.

As long as we walked through the narrow village streets, the walls blocked some of the wind. But now and then a sudden, swirling blast of sand would tear down the street, slamming into walls or battering the sides of houses before breaking apart into showers of dust.

Once we reached open ground, there was nothing to shield us. The full force of the khamseen hit us. It felt like it sucked the life right out of our bones and turned our bodies into dried-up sponges.

We didn't meet a single soul in the streets. Except for the howling of stray dogs under the moon, the village was completely silent.

The graveyard was surrounded by a tall mud wall. We stood under it for a few minutes, out of the wind, and quickly made a plan. A row of tamarisk trees ran through the middle of the cemetery, close to

Abdul's grave. We figured if we followed the wall on the outside and climbed over near the trees, the strong wind might help hide us if someone was already there.

We were about to move when the wind suddenly died down. In the silence, we clearly heard the sound of a shovel digging into the ground—and, even worse, the sharp cry of a carrion hawk circling overhead.

Two minutes later, we were creeping forward, using the tamarisk trees for cover. Big green beetles flew clumsily around, bumping into my face with loud clicks from their hard shells. When we got about twenty yards from the grave, we stopped and peeked out carefully from behind the trees.

There was a man waist-deep in the dirt, digging up Abdul's grave.

Weston, who was behind me, had already put on his "Spirit of Black Magic" costume, complete with fake eyes and teeth made from orange peel. When I turned and suddenly saw him, I nearly screamed—it was that convincing. Weston just shook with silent laughter and motioned for me to move closer. We slipped forward and now were only about twelve yards from the grave.

We waited there quietly for about ten minutes. The man digging, who we now clearly saw was Achmet, worked hard, completely naked. His brown skin glistened with sweat in the moonlight. Sometimes he muttered strange words to himself. Every now and then he stopped to rest. Then he scraped the dirt with his hands and rummaged through a pile of clothes nearby. He pulled out a rope and climbed into the grave.

In a moment, he was back up, pulling hard on the rope. A coffin started to appear. Achmet chipped a piece off the lid with his knife to make sure it was the right side. Then, setting it upright, he ripped off the top.

Leaning there in the moonlight was Abdul's small, shriveled body, tightly wrapped in white cloth like a baby.

I was about to tell Weston to jump out and scare Achmet, but then I remembered what Machmout had said: "He has Black Magic that can raise the dead."

My fear and disgust froze into pure curiosity.

"Wait," I whispered to Weston. "Let's see what happens."

The wind died again, and in the stillness, I heard the hawk's cry, even closer this time. I thought there were several birds now.

Meanwhile, Achmet unwrapped Abdul's face and untied the band around his chin, the one Arabs use to keep the mouth closed after death. I saw the jaw drop open as soon as the band was removed. Even after sixty hours of death, the body wasn't stiff. The wind carried the awful smell of decay toward us, but I was too fascinated to move.

Achmet didn't seem to mind the gaping mouth. He moved quickly, pulling two small black objects from his clothes. (Those objects, by the way, are now lying somewhere deep in the Nile mud.) He rubbed them together, and they started to glow with a sickly yellow light. A faint, ghostly flame rose between them.

He placed one glowing cube in the dead man's mouth and the other in his own. Then, holding Abdul's body tightly, he began to breathe into the dead man's mouth.

It was a horrifying sight.

Suddenly, Achmet jerked back with a gasp and froze. The cube in Abdul's mouth wasn't falling out—it was clenched tightly between the dead man's teeth.

After a moment's hesitation, Achmet rushed back to his clothes, grabbed his knife, and returned. Hiding the knife behind his back, he forced the cube from Abdul's mouth and spoke:

"Abdul," he said, "I am your friend. I swear I'll give your money to Mohamed if you tell me where it is."

I'm certain I saw Abdul's lips move and his eyelids flutter, like a wounded bird trying to fly.

The horror finally overwhelmed me, and I cried out without meaning to.

Achmet whipped around at the sound.

At the same moment, Weston—dressed as the Spirit of Black Magic—stepped out from the shadows. Achmet froze in terror, then turned to run—but stumbled and fell straight into the grave he had dug.

Weston dropped the fake eyes and teeth and turned on me in frustration.

"You ruined everything!" he said angrily. "It could have been the most incredible—"

He stopped mid-sentence.

He was staring at Abdul's body. Abdul had leaned forward out of the coffin, tottered, and fallen face-down onto the ground. For a second he lay there. Then, without any visible cause, he rolled onto his back and lay staring up at the sky.

His face was covered in dust, but I could see fresh blood mixed into it. A nail had caught the burial cloth and ripped it—and the clothes underneath—leaving his right shoulder bare.

Weston struggled to speak, then finally said:

"I'll go inform the police—if you'll stay here and make sure Achmet doesn't escape."

But I absolutely refused to stay alone.

Instead, we covered Abdul's body with the coffin lid to protect it from the hawks, tied up Achmet with the rope he had used, and marched him back to Luxor.

The next morning, Mohamed came to see us.

"I knew Achmet figured out where the money was!" he said proudly.

"Where was it?" we asked.

Mohamed pulled a small purse from his pocket.

"Tied around his shoulder," he said. "That dog had already started stripping it off. Look—here it is."

Inside were twenty English five-pound notes.

Weston and I had a slightly different theory. Even Weston agreed that Achmet had tried to use black magic to force the dead man to reveal the treasure's hiding place—and then planned to kill him again if needed. But that, of course, is just a guess.

There's one last strange thing: we had picked up the two black cubes Achmet used. They were covered with strange carvings. One evening, I handed them to Machmout while he was doing one of his "thought-transference" sessions.

The reaction was immediate—he screamed, shouting that the Black Magic had come.

Whether it really had or not, I wasn't taking any chances. I threw the cubes into the middle of the Nile.

Weston grumbled that he had wanted to send them to the British Museum—but I think he said that only after he realized they were gone.

The Shootings of Achnaleish

The dining room windows—one facing Oakley Street and the other looking out onto a tiny backyard with three sooty bushes (called "the garden")—were wide open, letting in what little air there was. But even with both windows open, the heat was unbearable. For once, July had actually remembered it was supposed to be hot. And hot it was—heat bounced off the walls, rose up from the pavement, and poured down from a huge sun that had been blazing in the sky all day.

Dinner was finished, but the four of us who had eaten were still sitting around the table.

Mabel Armytage—who had earlier said it was the "duty of good little summers to be hot"—was the first to speak.

“Oh, Jim, it sounds amazing,” she said. “Just thinking about it makes me feel cooler. Imagine—in just two weeks we’ll be there, all four of us, at our very own shooting lodge—"

“Farmhouse,” Jim corrected her.

“Well, I didn’t mean it was Balmoral," she said, "but still, our own little salmon river rushing down into our very own loch!”

Jim lit a cigarette.

“Mabel, you’re setting yourself up for disappointment,” he said. “It’s just a farmhouse—kind of a big one, but we’ll still be squeezing in. That ‘salmon river’ you’re dreaming of is really just a big stream. Sure, they say salmon have been caught there, but when I saw it, I thought it would be as hard for a salmon to fit into it as it’ll be for us to fit into that house. And the loch? It’s more like a pond.”

Mabel grabbed the Guide to Highland Shootings out of my hand—way rougher than even a sister should treat her older brother—and pointed an accusing finger at Jim.

"'Achnaleish,'" she read dramatically, "'is located in one of the grandest and most remote parts of Sutherlandshire. Available from August 12 through October, includes a lodge with shooting and fishing. Owner provides two keepers, a fishing guide, a boat on the loch, and dogs. Tenant can expect to shoot about 500 grouse and 500 other game, like partridges, black grouse, woodcock, snipe, and roe deer. Also lots of rabbits, especially by ferreting. The loch is full of brown trout, and when the river runs high, sea trout and the occasional salmon can be caught. Lodge includes'—I can't even go on, it's too hot. And the rent's only £350!"

Jim listened patiently.

"Well?" he said. "What's your point?"

Mabel stood up with as much dignity as the heat allowed.

"It is a shooting lodge with a salmon river and a loch, just like I said. Come on, Madge, let's get out of here. It's too hot to sit inside."

"You'll be calling Buxton 'the major-domo' next," Jim said as Mabel swept past him.

I picked the Guide to Highland Shootings back up—the one Mabel had yanked from me—and absentmindedly flipped through it, comparing Achnaleish to other properties.

"It actually seems cheap," I said. "Look—here's a similar place where the rent's £500. And another one at £550."

Jim poured himself a cup of coffee.

"Yeah, it does seem cheap," he agreed. "But it's way out there. It took me three hours to drive from Lairg—and that's without exactly sticking to the speed limit. But still, you're right—it's a bargain."

Now, my wife Madge has certain strong beliefs. One of them—an expensive one—is that anything cheap always has some hidden problem you only discover too late. With houses, she usually suspects either bad plumbing or terrible servant quarters. So I brought that up.

"Nope, the drains are fine," Jim said. "I even have an inspector's certificate. And honestly, the servants' quarters are probably nicer than ours. I really can't figure out why it's so cheap."

"Maybe the game numbers are exaggerated," I suggested.

Jim shook his head again.

"No, that's what's so strange. I think they actually understated it. When I walked around for a couple of hours, the whole moor was crawling with hares. You could easily shoot 500 hares alone."

"Hares?" I asked. "That's odd. Aren't they pretty rare that far north?"

Jim laughed.

"Exactly what I thought. And they're strange hares too—big, dark-colored ones. Anyway, let's go join the others outside. Good grief, what a hot night!"

Just like Mabel had said, two weeks later the four of us—who had been sweating and suffering in the heat of Chelsea—were speeding through the cool, refreshing winds of the North. The road was in perfect condition, and honestly, I wouldn't be surprised if Jim's big Napier wasn't exactly sticking to the speed limit for the second time.

The servants had already gone ahead, leaving the same day we did, while we got off the train at Perth, drove to Inverness, and were now, on the second day, getting close to our destination. I had never seen a road so empty—there probably wasn't even one person for every mile we drove.

We had left Lairg around five that afternoon, hoping to reach Achnaleish by eight. But disaster after disaster slowed us down. First, it was the engine, then a flat tire. Finally, about eight miles from the house, we stopped to turn on the headlights because thick clouds had rolled in from the west, and we lost the bright, clear northern twilight we were counting on.

We set off again, and after a few minutes, as the car bumped over a bridge, Jim said,

"That's the bridge over our salmon river. Keep an eye out for the turnoff to the lodge. It's to the right and only a narrow track. Go ahead and speed up, Sefton," he added to the driver. "We won't meet a soul."

I was sitting in front, and the speed and darkness were oddly exciting. Our headlights threw a bright circle of light ahead of us, fading sharply into blackness at the edges. Every now and then, something would dart across the light—a bird flapping away just in time, or a rabbit that panicked and darted onto the road before bouncing back again.

But most often it was hares. They would jump up from the grass and race ahead of us, confused and frightened by the light, too stunned to turn back into the darkness. I kept thinking we were about to hit one—they would barely leap out of the way just in time.

Then one sprang out almost under the car, and to my surprise, it was enormous—and it looked completely black. It ran ahead of us for a hundred yards, stuck in the headlights, then tried to swerve away—but too late. With a horrible jolt, we hit it.

Sefton immediately slowed the car and stopped. Jim had a strict rule: if they hit any animal, they always went back to make sure it wasn't suffering. Sefton jumped down and ran back.

"What was it?" Jim asked me while we waited.

"A hare," I said.

Sefton soon returned, carrying something.

"Yes, sir, it's dead," he said. "I picked it up, sir."

"Why?" Jim asked.

"Thought you might want to see it, sir. It's the biggest hare I ever saw—and it's black."

Right after that, we found the narrow track that led up to the house, and a few minutes later, we were inside.

It turned out that calling it just a "farmhouse" wasn't right either. The place was large, well-designed, and beautifully furnished. And judging by the happy look on Buxton's face—the head servant—the living quarters for the staff were excellent too.

The entrance hall had a big open fireplace and two tall bookcases filled with serious books, the kind you'd expect from an educated minister. Coming downstairs, dressed for dinner before the others, I browsed the shelves and immediately grabbed a book that seemed to match a vague thought in my head: Elwes's Folklore of the Northwest Highlands.

I flipped to the index, found "Hare," and read:

"It is not only witches who are believed to change into animals. Ordinary men and women are thought to have this power too, especially turning into hares. They can be recognized by their unusually large size and nearly jet-black color."

The next morning, I woke up early, eager to explore the new place.

I had expected the house to be completely isolated, but I was wrong. Just half a mile away, down the steep slope where the house sat on top, was a small village—a typical Scottish village street, probably the hamlet of Achnaleish. Because of the steep hill, the village felt far away, even though it wasn't. There were at least four dozen houses—more people than we had seen since we left Lairg.

About a mile away, I could see the shining surface of the sea, and on the other side, away from the village, I spotted the river and the loch. The house itself was perched on a high ridge—you had to climb uphill from every direction to reach it. But like all Scottish homes, no matter how small, it had bright flowers decorating the walls: purple clematis and orange tropaeolum vines made it feel cheerful and welcoming.

It all looked calm and peaceful.

I wandered around for a while and came back late for breakfast. I found out there had been a small hiccup in the morning plans: the head gamekeeper, Maclaren, hadn't shown up. His assistant, Sandie Ross, told us why—Maclaren's mother had died suddenly the night before.

She hadn't been sick. She was just getting ready for bed when she suddenly threw up her arms, screamed like she was terrified, and collapsed, dead.

Sandie, a slow-spoken and polite Scottish man, told me this quietly after breakfast while we stood outside the back door.

At that moment, Sefton, the smart-looking English chauffeur, came walking up from the stables. In one hand, he was carrying the black hare.

He tipped his hat as he passed me.

"Just bringing it up for Mr. Armytage to see, sir," he said. "She's as black as a boot."

Sefton turned into the house, but not before Sandie Ross caught a glimpse of what he was carrying. Suddenly, the usually slow and polite Scotsman looked nervous and suspicious.

"And where might you have found that, sir?" he asked.

By then, I was already getting curious about the black-hare superstition.

"Why do you want to know?" I asked him.

Sandie tried to pull himself together, forcing his usual calm look back onto his face.

"It's no concern of mine," he said. "I just asked. There's a lot of black hares in Achnaleish."

But he couldn't hold back for long.

"That hare you found—it was near the road leading up to Achnaleish, wasn't it?"

"Yes," I said. "We found it right on the road."

Sandie turned away quickly.

"She always sat there," he muttered.

Later that morning, we went out for some casual shooting. The steep hill between our house and the moor was dotted with small woods, and we spent the morning walking through them with a random group of beaters. Even Buxton, the butler, was among them.

We had decent luck, but strangely, we didn't see any of the hares that Jim had said were everywhere. Finally, just before lunch, a large dark-colored hare darted out from the top of one of the woods about thirty yards from Jim. He hesitated for a second—he's careful about taking long or risky shots at hares—but then raised his gun to shoot.

At that exact moment, Sandie, who had been standing nearby after giving orders to the beaters, suddenly rushed forward. With amazing speed, he struck up the barrels of Jim's gun with his stick before he could pull the trigger.

"Black hare!" he shouted. "You'd shoot a black hare? There's no shooting hares at Achnaleish, and don't you forget it!"

The look on Sandie's face was incredible, like he had just stopped a thief from stabbing someone.

"And with the sickness around too!" he added angrily. "When poor folk finally get a break from their fevered bodies, they go to the cool moors!"

Then he caught himself, realizing how much he had blurted out.

"I'm sorry, sir," he said more calmly to Jim. "I got upset. What with one thing and another—and the black hare you found dead last night—ach, I'm babbling again. But there's no shooting hares in Achnaleish, that's certain."

Jim was still standing there in total shock when I walked up. Even though I love shooting, I'm just as interested in folklore, so I spoke up.

"But we've rented the hunting rights to Achnaleish, Sandie," I said. "There was nothing in the agreement about not shooting hares."

Sandie's temper flared again.

"And maybe there was nothing about shooting the women and children either!" he shouted.

I glanced around. All the beaters had finished coming through the woods. Buxton and Jim's valet stood apart from the others, but the rest gathered close, hanging onto every word. They whispered to each other now and then in Gaelic, which somehow made me even more uneasy.

"But what do hares have to do with the women and children of Achnaleish?" I asked.

No real answer came, just the same repeated line: "There's no shooting hares in Achnaleish, whatever happens." Then Sandie turned stiffly to Jim.

"That's the end of the wood, sir," he said. "We've been all around."

Despite the weirdness, the morning's hunt had actually gone very well. Jim had shot a roe deer (I should have shot one too, but missed), and we had a good haul: a dozen black-game, four pigeons, six pairs of grouse, about thirty rabbits, and four pairs of woodcock. This was just from the small woods near the house—we hadn't even gone up to the moors yet. But that was all we had planned for the morning anyway, since our wives had requested a fishing lesson that afternoon.

Sandie had organized the beat really well, leaving us just a couple hundred yards from the house by a few minutes to two o'clock.

After a quick glance at me, Jim spoke to Sandie, changing the subject completely.

"Well, the beat went great," he said. "This afternoon we'll be fishing. Pay the beaters their wages each evening, and just tell me the total. Thanks, everyone."

We walked back toward the house. The moment our backs were turned, a loud buzz of whispering broke out behind us. I glanced back and saw Sandie and the beaters huddled together, talking quickly.

Jim turned to me.

"This is more your department than mine," he said. "I prefer shooting hares to digging up ridiculous superstitions about why I shouldn't. What does it all mean?"

I told him about what I had read in Elwes's Folklore of the Northwest Highlands the night before.

"So do they think we killed the old woman on the road? And that I was about to kill someone else this morning?" Jim asked, half-laughing. "How do we know they won't start saying the rabbits are their cousins and the grouse are their children? I've never heard such nonsense. Tomorrow we'll have a proper hare drive. Forget the grouse. We'll settle this hare issue first."

Jim was now in full stubborn Englishman mode. In his mind, he had paid to hunt at Achnaleish, and if that included hares, then nothing—not superstition, not warnings—was going to stop him.

"Then there's going to be a real row," I warned.

Jim just snorted.

At lunch, we finally found out what Sandie had meant earlier when he talked about the "sickness."

"Imagine that awful influenza reaching a place like this," Madge said. "Mabel and I went down to the village this morning. Ted, you wouldn't believe it—you can buy anything there, from raincoats to peppermints. Anyway, there was a sick-looking child in the shop. We asked about it, and all they said was, 'It's the sickness.' But from what the woman told us, it's clearly influenza—sudden fever and all the usual signs."

"Is it a bad kind?" I asked.

"Yes. A few old people have already died from pneumonia after getting it."

Now, I do believe in standing up for my rights as an Englishman. But if a mad bull blocks my way across a field, I don't insist on crossing it. I simply go around, because there's no point arguing with a bull about my constitutional rights.

That afternoon, while Madge and I floated around the loch in a boat—and while I kept busy untangling her fishing lines from her hair, my jacket, and itself—I thought about our situation with the people of Achnaleish and the hares. It seemed a lot like the bull and the field.

Jim technically had the right to shoot hares at Achnaleish, just like I would technically have the right to walk through a bull's field. But it was just as hopeless to try convincing the villagers that their hares weren't anything special. They truly believed the hares were the souls of their friends and relatives, not just animals. You couldn't argue that away with a five-minute talk—it would probably take a few generations of education to even start.

Right now, this wasn't superstition to them—it was a serious belief. I saw it in the horror on Sandie's face when Jim tried to shoot that hare. And now, with a dangerous flu spreading through the village, Jim was planning a hare-drive tomorrow. What could possibly go wrong?

That night, Jim ranted about it in the smoking-room.

"But really, what can they do?" he cried. "What if some old man from Achnaleish says I shot his granddaughter? And when asked for proof, he says we ate her but he kept the skin for evidence—and the 'skin' turns out to be a hare's skin? I mean, folklore is fine for conversation when there's nothing else to talk about, but don't tell me it can mess with real life! What can they actually do?"

"They could shoot us," I said.

"The good, God-fearing Scots shoot us for shooting hares?" he scoffed.

"Well, it's possible. But even if they don't, you won't get much of a hare-drive going."

"Why not?"

"Because you won't find a single local willing to beat for you. No beaters, no keepers. You'll have to go yourself, with just Buxton and your man."

"Then I'll fire Sandie," Jim snapped.

"That would be a shame—he's good at his job."

Jim stood up, still fuming.

"Well, his job tomorrow will be to drive hares for you and me," he said. "Or are you chickening out?"

"I'm chickening out," I said honestly.

The next morning, things happened fast. Jim and I got up early and found Sandie waiting quietly by the back door. About a dozen young Highlanders who had helped us the day before were hanging around in the yard.

"Good morning, Sandie," said Jim, briskly. "Today we're driving hares. We should get a bunch up in those gullies above. See if you can get another dozen beaters."

"There'll be no hare-drive here," Sandie said calmly.

"I gave you an order," Jim said sharply.

Sandie turned to the beaters and said a few words in Gaelic. Instantly, they all bolted, running full speed down the hill toward the village. One paused at the top of the slope to wave his arms, signaling the others, I guessed.

Then Sandie faced Jim again.

"Where are your beaters now, sir?" he asked.

For a moment, I thought Jim was going to punch him. But he kept control.

"You're fired," he said.

Without beaters or a keeper—Maclaren had the day off to bury his mother—the hare-drive was clearly impossible. Jim, still blustering a bit but clearly shaken by how quickly the beaters had deserted, grumbled that they'd probably all come crawling back by tomorrow.

Meanwhile, something else odd was happening. The post, which usually came early, hadn't arrived. But Mabel had seen the post-cart coming up the drive a while ago.

I got a hunch and ran to the edge of the ridge where the house sat. Sure enough, the post-cart was heading away from the house without dropping off our letters.

Back inside the dining-room, more problems piled up: the bread was stale, the milk was sour, and Buxton was called to explain. Turns out, neither the milkman nor the baker had shown up that morning.

From a folk-lore perspective, this was actually fascinating.

"There's an old superstition called a 'taboo,'" I said. "It means no one will sell you anything or give you any service."

“My dear fellow, a little knowledge is a dangerous thing,” Jim said, reaching for the marmalade.

I just laughed.

"You’re upset," I said, "because you’re starting to wonder if there’s actually something to all this."

"Yes, that’s true," Jim admitted. "But who would have thought there could be anything real in it? Oh, come on—there can’t be. A hare is just a hare."

"Unless it’s your first cousin," I said.

"Then I’ll just go out and shoot some first cousins by myself," he said.

Thankfully, we talked him out of that plan. Instead, he went with Madge down by the stream, and I spent the morning hidden in a thick patch of bushes on the hill above Achnaleish, watching the village through my field-glasses. From there, the view was so clear it was like looking at a map.

First, there was a funeral—probably Maclaren’s mother’s. It seemed like the whole village attended. But after the service, nobody went back to their work. It was as if it were Sunday. People just stood around in groups, talking quietly. Now and then one group would break apart, but the people would just drift over to join another. No one went into their homes or out to the fields.

Right before lunchtime, I had an idea and decided to test it. I ran down the hill and walked into the street, pretending nothing was wrong. Sandie was there, but he turned his back on me completely. Everyone else did too. Whenever I came near a group, their talking would instantly stop. They didn’t just stand around anymore either—they started moving off quietly, one by one, heading toward their houses.

I saw the shop—the one Mabel had called "the heavenly shop"—at the end of the street. Its door was open and a small child stood there, looking out. I walked toward it, planning to go in, buy something, and try to start a conversation. But just as I got close, a man inside quickly pulled the child away, slammed the door, and locked it.

I knocked. I rang the bell. No answer. Only the sound of the child crying from behind the door.

The once-busy street was now deserted. It looked like a ghost town, except for a few wisps of smoke rising from chimneys. It was so quiet you could hear your own heart beating. But even though I couldn't see anyone, I knew I was being watched—watched from behind the windows, watched with eyes full of mistrust and hate.

It sent a cold shiver down my spine. Being stared at by people you can't see is bad enough. Knowing they all hate you makes it much worse.

I climbed back up to my hiding spot and looked down again. The street was busy once more.

All of this made me nervous. Clearly, the taboo was real now: no one would talk to us, sell to us, or even acknowledge us. But why were they holding these secretive meetings? What else were they planning?

That afternoon, I found out.

Around two o'clock, the villagers finally stopped gathering in groups. But instead of going back to their homes, they all—men, women, and children—spread out across the hills in little groups of two or three. At first, I thought they were just getting back to their normal work. I watched a woman and a girl cutting dead bracken and heather, gathering it up.

It seemed normal enough. I looked around at other groups. Again and again, I saw the same thing.

They were all cutting fuel. Everyone.

Then, all at once, an idea hit me. It seemed crazy—but it hit again, stronger this time. I didn't wait to think more. I scrambled out of my hiding place and rushed to find Jim by the stream.

I told him exactly what I had seen—and what I thought it meant. And I think that, at that moment, Jim's disbelief in folk-lore started to waver.

Less than fifteen minutes later, the chauffeur and I were speeding down the road to Lairg in the Napier, going as fast as the car could manage. We hadn't told the women what I suspected. We didn't want to scare them—and we believed that, with the plans we were making, there was no real danger.

We set up a private signal: if my guess turned out to be right, Jim would place a light in the window of my room. That way, I would see it when I came back after dark from Lairg.

Officially, I was just going to town to pick up some fishing flies.

As we sped toward Lairg in the big car—it really felt more like gliding than driving—I kept thinking everything over. By now, I was sure: the villagers had been gathering wood and brush to pile around our house and set on fire after dark. We figured they would wait until late, probably until they thought we were all asleep.

I needed to find out if the police at Lairg agreed with my theory. That's why I was heading there as fast as I could.

When I arrived, I told the chief constable everything, making sure not to leave anything out or exaggerate. As I talked, his face grew more and more serious.

"You did the right thing coming here," he said. "The people at Achnaleish are some of the toughest and wildest in all of Scotland. But you'll have to stop hunting hares," he added.

He picked up the phone.

"I'll get five men together," he said. "We'll be ready in ten minutes."

Our plan was simple. We would leave the car out of sight so the villagers wouldn't know we were there. If I saw the signal—a light in my window—we would sneak up from all sides and surround the house. It wouldn't be too hard to move unseen through the woods nearby. Hiding just at the edges, we would wait and watch to see if the villagers piled brushwood around the lodge. If anyone came to light it, we'd catch them right away.

It was about ten o'clock when we got out of the car and started sneaking toward the house. I saw the signal—the light burning in my window—and the rest of the house looked completely still.

Since I didn't have a weapon, after helping the men get into position around the house, I went back to wait with Sergeant Duncan behind a hedge near the garden.

I don't know how long we waited. It felt endless. Every so often an owl would hoot, or a rabbit would dart out to nibble the grass. The night sky was heavy with clouds, and the house stood like a dark shadow, with just a few narrow slits of light where windows were still glowing. After a while, even those lights went out, and the house looked completely lifeless.

Then, out of nowhere, it happened. I heard the scrape of a foot on the gravel. A flash of lantern light appeared.

Duncan shouted, "Move a muscle and I'll shoot! My gun's aimed right at you!"

I blew my whistle. The others rushed in, and within a minute it was over.

The man we caught was Maclaren.

"They killed my mother with that devil-car," he said. "She was just sitting by the road. She never hurt anyone."

And that, to him, was a good enough reason to try to burn us alive.

It took some time to break into the house because they had carefully wired shut all the doors and windows on the ground floor. They had clearly planned everything very carefully.

Technically, we still had the rental of Achnaleish for two more months. But after that night, none of us really wanted to stay if it meant risking our lives. We didn't want to send Maclaren to prison either. What we really wanted was simple: peace, food deliveries, and some help for our hunting trips.

So we made a deal. We would stop shooting hares, and Maclaren would be released. A meeting the next morning settled everything.

The two months that followed turned out to be wonderful. Everyone got along just fine after that.

But if anyone wants to see how real "old legends" can be, I suggest they try shooting hares at Achnaleish.

How Fear Departed from the Long Gallery

Church-Peveril is a house so full of ghosts—both ones you can see and ones you can hear—that the family who lives there doesn't even take them seriously anymore. For the Peverils, seeing a ghost is about as normal as getting the mail is for everyone else. Ghosts show up almost every day, making noises, knocking, or walking up the driveway. I've even seen Mrs. Peveril herself, who can't see very well, squint into the evening shadows as we drank coffee on the terrace and say to her daughter:

"My dear, wasn't that the Blue Lady going into the bushes? I hope she won't scare Flo. Whistle for her, dear."

(Flo, by the way, is the youngest and most spoiled of their many dachshunds.)

Blanche Peveril gave a lazy whistle and crunched the sugar at the bottom of her coffee cup with her white teeth.

"Oh, darling, Flo isn't silly enough to be scared," she said. "Poor Aunt Barbara in her blue dress is such a bore! Every time I meet her, she looks like she wants to say something. But when I ask, 'What is it, Aunt Barbara?' she just points toward the house. I think she had something to confess about two hundred years ago, but now she's forgotten it."

Right then, Flo barked happily and danced around what looked to me like an empty patch of lawn.

"There! Flo's made friends with her," said Mrs. Peveril. "I do wonder why she wears that awful shade of blue."

From this, you can see that the Peverils are very used to ghosts. They don't exactly make fun of them—after all, they only look down on people who hate hunting, shooting, golf, or skating—but they definitely don't get spooked. Since all their ghosts are family members, they figure even the poor Blue Lady must have been good at sports once.

In fact, they're very fond of one ghost: Master Anthony. He was a terrible man in life, but he was also a fantastic horseman. He died trying to ride a horse up the main staircase after doing something awful in the garden. When Blanche comes down in the morning looking extra cheerful and announces that Master Anthony was "very loud" last night, everyone smiles. They take it as a sign that he's still full of energy.

If you're lucky enough to stay at Church-Peveril, they'll put you in a haunted bedroom as a compliment. It shows they think you're worthy. They'll warn you that great-great-grandma Bridget sometimes messes around by the fireplace but that it's best not to talk to her, and that you might hear Master Anthony on the staircase before dawn.

At night, you'll undress nervously in a huge, drafty room where the firelight dances over tapestries showing grim hunts and battles. You'll climb into a bed so enormous it feels like you're sleeping in the desert and pray for morning. All the while, you're half-sure that Freddy, Harry, Blanche, or even Mrs. Peveril might sneak around dressed up as ghosts to scare you. Personally, I always claim I have a weak heart and insist on sleeping in the modern wing where no ghosts go.

I can't remember all the details about great-great-grandma Bridget, except that she once cut the throat of a distant cousin and then killed herself with an axe that had been used at the Battle of Agincourt. Her life was full of wild stories.

But there's one haunting at Church-Peveril that no one jokes about. It's not funny, and it's not a family sport. It's deadly serious. The family only talks about it as much as necessary to warn their guests.

It's not one ghost, but two—the ghosts of twin children.

Mrs. Peveril told me their story:

In 1602, toward the end of Queen Elizabeth's reign, Dick Peveril, a handsome younger brother of Joseph Peveril, was a favorite at court. Joseph, who owned the family house, had twin boys very late in life at seventy-four. Queen Elizabeth once told Dick, "It's a pity you're not master of Church-Peveril," which might have given him terrible ideas.

Dick rode north toward Yorkshire just as Joseph, weakened by the heat and too much wine, suddenly died of a stroke. Dick arrived just in time for the funeral. He stayed on to comfort Joseph's widow, a timid woman not fit for the ruthless Peverils.

On the second night, Dick did something the family still regrets today. He went into the room where the twins slept with their nurse, strangled the nurse as she slept, and took the two toddlers to the giant fireplace in the long gallery. The weather had turned cold, and the fire was piled high with burning logs. In the middle of that roaring fire, Dick threw the children, stamping them down with his riding boots when they tried to move. They were too small to escape.

It's said he laughed as he piled more logs on top of them.

That's how Dick Peveril became the master of Church-Peveril.

The crime was never officially pinned on him, but handsome Dick didn't get to enjoy his bloody inheritance for long. Within a year, he was dying. As he lay on his deathbed, he confessed everything to the priest by his side. But before he could be forgiven, he died.

That same night, the haunting began—the one the Peveril family still barely speaks of, and only in whispers. Just an hour or two after Dick died, one of the servants walking past the long gallery heard loud laughter from inside. It was the same cheerful but eerie laugh they thought they would never hear again.

Gathering his courage, the servant opened the door, expecting to see the ghost of Dick himself. Instead, he saw two tiny figures in white nightgowns, holding hands and toddling toward him across the moonlit floor.

The people who were keeping watch over Dick's body heard a loud crash and rushed upstairs. They found the servant lying in the middle of the gallery, frozen by a terrible seizure. Near dawn, he woke up just long enough to tell what he had seen. Then, pointing with a shaking, grey finger toward the door, he let out a scream—and died.

Over the next fifty years, the legend of the ghostly twins became more and more feared. Thankfully for the family, the twins only appeared rarely—maybe four or five times during that whole period. But whenever they did, it was always the same: at night, between sunset and sunrise, always in the long gallery, and always appearing as two tiny children who could barely walk.

Each time, the person who saw them died soon after. Some lived a few months before they died in terror; others, like the first servant, didn't last more than a few hours.

The worst story of all was what happened to Mrs. Canning in 1760.

By then, everyone knew about the danger of the long gallery. Visitors were warned not to go there at night. But Mrs. Canning, who was a famous beauty and very clever, laughed at all the warnings. She was friends with the famous skeptic Voltaire and thought the whole idea was silly.

So night after night, she sat alone in the gallery, waiting to see the ghosts. Four nights went by with nothing happening. But on the fifth night, she finally saw them: the door opened, and the two ghostly toddlers walked toward her.

Even then, she didn't seem scared. Instead, she mocked them, telling them it was time for them to crawl back into the fire. The children didn't answer. They just turned away, crying.

Later, she came downstairs, proud and excited, telling everyone she had seen the ghosts and would write to Voltaire about it—thinking it would make him laugh.

But when the full story reached Voltaire months later, he didn't laugh at all.

Mrs. Canning had been one of the most admired women of her time. She was 30 years old in 1760 and still had the flawless skin of a young girl. She loved being out in bright sunlight, which most women avoided, because it made her glowing complexion look even more beautiful.

That's why, about two weeks after her encounter with the twins, she was so alarmed when she noticed a small grey spot on her left cheek, just under her bright blue eyes.

She tried every lotion and treatment she could find, but nothing helped. She stayed hidden away, hoping to cure it. Instead, the spot grew larger.

Soon strange greenish-grey tendrils began to sprout from the center of the patch, like tiny plants. Another patch appeared on her lower lip. One morning she woke up to find her vision blurry. Rushing to the mirror, she screamed: a new growth had appeared under her upper eyelid, covering her eye with thin, mushroom-like threads.

After that, her tongue and throat became infected. Her breathing grew harder and harder. In the end, she died by suffocation—a mercy, given the terrible suffering she had endured.

Even worse was the fate of Colonel Blantyre, who had tried to shoot the ghostly children with his revolver. The horrors he went through were so awful that they were never fully written down.

The Peverils take this haunting very seriously. Every guest who stays at the house is warned as soon as they arrive: no one is allowed to enter the long gallery after sunset, no matter the reason.

During the day, though, the long gallery is a lovely room and deserves a description, especially since it's important to understand its layout for what happens next. The gallery is about eighty feet long, with six tall windows along one side that overlook the gardens. One door leads to the main staircase landing, and halfway down the opposite wall, another door connects to the back staircase and the servants' area. The gallery is often used as a shortcut for the servants heading to rooms on the first floor.

It was through this back door that the ghostly children came when they appeared to Mrs. Canning. They've also been seen entering there on other occasions, because the room where handsome Dick took them from lies just beyond the top of the back stairs. Further down the gallery is the fireplace where Dick burned them, and at the far end, there's a big bow-window that looks straight down the main avenue.

Hanging above the fireplace is a chilling portrait of handsome Dick as a young man, painted with all his bold good looks. It's said to be by

Holbein. Around the room are a dozen more portraits, all of great quality.

During the day, the gallery is filled with life and laughter. The ghosts never show themselves in the daylight, and the creepy sound of Dick's sinister laugh—which passersby sometimes hear after dark—is completely absent. But if Blanche happens to hear it in the evening, she doesn't smile; she quickly covers her ears and hurries away from the sound.

In the daytime, though, the gallery is lively and cheerful. In the summer, people lounge in the deep window seats. In winter, when the cold wind blows, they gather around the fireplace at the far end, sitting on sofas, chairs, and even the floor, laughing and chatting.

I've spent many long August afternoons there, staying until it was nearly time to get dressed for dinner. But no one ever stays too late. As the sun begins to set, someone always says, "It's getting close to sunset—shall we go?"

Later in the year, when the days are shorter, they sometimes have tea in the gallery. But even then, no matter how loud the laughter gets, there's always a moment when Mrs. Peveril glances out the window and says, "It's getting late, my dears. Let's move downstairs." At her words, a sudden quiet falls over everyone, as if bad news had been announced, and we all silently leave. Still, the living Peverils are naturally cheerful, and any gloom quickly fades once we're downstairs.

Not long after Christmas last year, the house was full of young, lively guests. Mrs. Peveril, as always, was planning her big New Year's Eve ball on December 31st.

The house was packed, and she even had to book extra rooms at the Peveril Arms, the local inn, to fit everyone.

For several days there had been a hard frost with no wind, which meant no hunting—but the frozen lake had turned into a perfect skating rink. Everyone had spent that morning skating, racing and doing tricks on the ice. After a quick lunch, nearly everyone rushed back outside to skate some more.

The only one who didn't join us was Madge Dalrymple. She had taken a bad fall earlier that day and hurt her knee. Hoping to rest it enough to dance at the ball later, she stayed inside. Honestly, her hope was pretty optimistic—she could barely limp back to the house. But with the cheerful spirit the Peverils are known for (she was Blanche's first cousin), she joked that missing more skating wasn't a big loss if it meant she might still be able to enjoy the evening.

After a quick cup of coffee, which we drank in the long gallery, we left Madge resting comfortably on the big sofa near the fireplace, with an interesting book to pass the time until tea.

Since she was family, Madge knew all about the story of handsome Dick, the ghostly babies, and the tragic fates of Mrs. Canning and Colonel Blantyre. As we were leaving, I heard Blanche tell her, "Don't cut it too close, dear," and Madge answered, "No, I'll leave well before sunset."

And with that, we left her alone in the long gallery.

Madge tried reading her book for a few minutes, but she couldn't really focus on it. She set it down and limped over to the window. Even though it was still early—just after two o'clock—the light outside was already dim and gloomy. The clear, bright morning had disappeared, replaced by heavy clouds moving slowly in from the northeast. The whole sky was covered now, and a few snowflakes were starting to drift past the tall windows.

Looking out into the cold, dark afternoon, Madge had a strong feeling that a heavy snowstorm was coming. The weather seemed to press down on her, making her feel drowsy and slow, the way she always did when a storm was near. She was very sensitive to changes in the weather—a sunny morning could fill her with energy, but when bad weather was coming, it made her feel heavy and tired.

Moving slowly, Madge limped back to the big sofa near the fire. The house was heated by water pipes, and although the fire had been allowed to burn low, the room was still very warm. She stretched out on the sofa, facing the fireplace, not bothering to pick up her book again. She planned to go to her room soon and spend the time writing a few letters before everyone came back from skating.

Lying there, she started to think sleepily about what she wanted to write. She had a letter overdue to her mother, who loved hearing about all the ghostly happenings at Church-Peveril. She would tell her how Master Anthony had been making loud noises on the stairs the other night, and how Mrs. Peveril had seen the Blue Lady that very morning walking through the garden. Mrs. Peveril had watched the Blue Lady enter the stables, and at that exact moment, all the horses had panicked—whinnying, kicking, and sweating in fear.

There had been no sightings of the haunted twins for many years, but everyone knew the long gallery was never used after dark. Madge sat up for a second, remembering that she was in the long gallery now. But when she checked her watch, she saw it was only a little after half-past two. If she left in about half an hour, she would have plenty of time to write her letters before tea.

She thought about picking up her book again but realized it was still sitting on the window ledge, and she felt far too lazy to get it. She was incredibly sleepy.

The sofa she was lying on had recently been re-covered in thick, soft velvet—a greyish-green color that reminded her of lichen. She stretched her arms out on either side, pressing her fingers into the soft material.

A horrible thought floated into her mind: the story of Mrs. Canning and how the strange lichen-like growth had taken over her body. Without any real break in her thoughts, Madge drifted off to sleep.

She dreamed.

In her dream, she thought she had woken up, still lying exactly where she had fallen asleep. The fire had flared up again, and the flickering light danced across the walls, lighting up the portrait of handsome Dick above the fireplace.

In the dream, she remembered everything perfectly—how she had hurt her knee, why she was inside instead of skating, and how she had planned to write letters. She tried to sit up to go to her room but caught sight of her arms stretched out on the sofa.

She couldn't tell where her fingers ended and where the velvet began. Her wrists and the blue veins on the backs of her hands were clear, but her fingers seemed to have melted into the grey fabric.

In her dream, she remembered again the awful story about Mrs. Canning and the strange growth that had covered her face, her eyes, and even her throat. Terror gripped her. She realized she was slowly turning into the sofa itself, becoming part of the grey velvet. She couldn't move. Soon the grey would cover her whole body. When the others came back from skating, they would find only a huge, lumpy cushion—and that would be all that was left of her.

The horror grew until, by a massive effort, she shook herself awake.

For a few minutes, she lay there, feeling only the huge relief that she was awake. She moved her fingers through the soft velvet, reassuring herself she was real. But even though she had shaken off the dream, she was still incredibly sleepy.

She lay there until she noticed something else—she could no longer see her hands at all. It had grown nearly dark.

Just then, a flare of flame shot up from the dying fire, lighting the room with a sudden, ghostly glow. The portrait of handsome Dick glared down at her, and for a moment, she could see her hands again.

Then the real panic began. The daylight was completely gone, and she realized she was all alone in the long gallery—in the dark.

She was frozen with fear, unable to move. But this was worse than a nightmare because she was awake, and fully aware. And now she understood why she was so afraid.

She knew—without any doubt—that she was about to see the twin babies.

Sweat broke out on her face, even as her mouth and throat went dry. Her tongue scraped against her teeth. She couldn't move a muscle. She just stared into the darkness with wide, terrified eyes.

The fire sputtered and died back again, and complete darkness closed in around her.

Across the room, on the wall facing the windows, a faint red glow started to appear. For a moment, Madge thought it was the sign that the terrible vision was coming. But then hope sparked inside her—she remembered the thick clouds covering the sky before she fell asleep and guessed that this reddish light might just be the last bit of sunset. That sudden hope gave her strength, and she jumped off the sofa.

She rushed to the window and saw a dull, glowing line on the horizon. But before she could move further, the glow disappeared behind the thick clouds again. A tiny flicker came from the fireplace, just enough to shine faintly on the tiles, and she heard snow tapping against the windows. Other than that, there was no light, no sound—only darkness.

Still, she had regained a little courage, enough to move. She started feeling her way down the gallery. But very quickly, she realized she was lost. She bumped into a chair, steadied herself, and then immediately ran into another. Next, a table blocked her path. She turned to avoid it and smacked right into the back of a sofa. She spun around again, only to see the faint firelight now on the opposite side from where she expected it. In her confusion, she must have turned herself completely around.

She had no idea which way to go now. It felt like furniture was everywhere, boxing her in. Meanwhile, the terrifying thought never left her mind—that the ghostly twin babies could appear at any moment.

Madge tried to pray. "Lighten our darkness, O Lord," she whispered, but she couldn't remember how the prayer went after that. She only knew there was something about "the perils of the night."

All the while she kept stretching her hands out in front of her, fluttering blindly through the dark. The little bit of firelight that should have been on her left now glowed faintly on her right. She turned herself again and kept repeating aloud, "Lighten our darkness," hoping the words would somehow protect her.

She stumbled into a screen—a piece of furniture she didn't remember being there. She quickly felt around it with her hands and touched something soft and velvety. Was it the sofa she had been lying on? If so, where was the back of it? It felt like something alive now, not a sofa at all—something soft, something wrong, like the lichen-colored velvet she had dreamed of.

Then panic took over completely. She could think of nothing but praying. She was lost—trapped in a dark place where nothing good could come, only the crying babies of legend. Her voice rose without her meaning to. From whispering, she began speaking, and from speaking, she started screaming. She shrieked the prayer again and again as she stumbled through the dark, crashing into tables, chairs, all the normal things of everyday life that had now turned terrible and strange.

Then—suddenly—came a horrible answer to her cries. Another hidden pocket of gas caught fire in the hearth, and for a few brief seconds, the room flared into light. She saw the cruel, mocking face of handsome Dick staring down at her from his portrait. She saw thick snowflakes falling outside.

And she saw exactly where she was: standing right in front of the door—the very door through which the ghostly twins were said to appear.

The flame sputtered out again, plunging her back into blackness. But now she had something she hadn't had before: she knew her way. She had seen that the middle of the room was clear. One quick dash straight ahead would take her to the door that led to the main staircase, and to safety. She had even seen the brass doorknob gleaming in the firelight, like a bright little star.

She could make it—it would only take a few seconds if she ran now.

She drew a deep breath, partly to calm herself, partly to steady her pounding heart. But just as she filled her lungs halfway, she froze again in terror.

She heard it—a faint whisper, just a tiny sound, coming from the door behind her. The door through which the twins entered.

She could see that the door was slowly opening. In the slight light from outside, she saw two little white figures standing there.

They started moving toward her, shuffling slowly across the floor.

She couldn't see their faces clearly. She couldn't even make out the details of their forms. But she knew—knew beyond all doubt—that these were the twin babies, the terrible spirits tied to the curse of the house.

For a moment, panic and despair fought inside her. But then, with a sudden rush of clear thought, she decided what to do.

She hadn't harmed them. She hadn't mocked them, like Mrs. Canning had. These were just innocent babies, murdered long ago. Maybe, just maybe, if she showed she meant no harm, they would spare her. After all, she was of their blood, a Peveril too. Maybe they would understand.

She hesitated only for a second. Then she dropped to her knees and stretched her hands toward them.

"Oh, my dears," she said softly, "I only fell asleep. I didn't mean to do anything wrong."

She paused, her heart aching with pity. In that moment, she thought not of herself but of them—these poor, innocent children, cursed to bring fear and death instead of joy and laughter.

No one before had pitied them—everyone had either feared them or mocked them.

And as that thought bloomed in her heart, the crushing fear that had frozen her melted away, just like the tight bud of a flower unfolding into spring sunlight.

"My dears, I'm so sorry for you," Madge said. "It's not your fault that you have to bring me whatever you do. But I'm not scared anymore. I only feel sorry for you. God bless you, poor little ones."

She raised her head and looked at them. Even though it was still very dark, she could now clearly see their faces. Everything looked a little blurry and shaky, like the flicker of weak flames moving in the wind. But their faces didn't look sad or angry—they smiled at her, shy and sweet like real babies.

As she watched, their little figures slowly faded away, disappearing like mist on a cold morning.

Madge didn't move right away. Instead of feeling afraid, she was filled with a deep sense of peace, so calming that she didn't want to move and risk losing it. She stayed there, still and quiet, for a little while. Then, slowly and calmly, she stood up.

She carefully made her way out of the long gallery, but now there was no fear chasing her, no panic rushing her steps.

When she reached the stairs, she saw Blanche coming up, swinging her skates and whistling happily.

"How's your leg, dear?" Blanche asked. "You're not limping anymore."

Until then, Madge hadn't even thought about her leg.

"I think it's fine," she said. "I had completely forgotten about it. Blanche, don't be scared for me—but I saw the twins."

For a second, Blanche's face went pale with shock.

"What?" she whispered.

"Yes, I just saw them," said Madge. "But they were kind. They smiled at me, and I felt so sorry for them. I really believe I have nothing to fear."

It turned out Madge was right. Nothing bad ever happened to her afterward.

It seems that her kindness and sympathy for the twins broke the terrible curse that had haunted Church-Peveril for so long.

In fact, just last week I visited the house again, arriving after dark. As I was passing the gallery door, Blanche came out.

"There you are," she said. "I just saw the twins. They looked so sweet—and they stayed almost ten minutes this time. Let's go have tea."

Caterpillars

A month or two ago, I read in an Italian newspaper that the Villa Cascana, where I once stayed, had been torn down. A factory was being built on the land where it used to stand. Because of that, I no longer feel any need to hold back from sharing what I saw—or thought I saw—at that house, or from mentioning the strange things that happened afterward, which might have been connected.

The Villa Cascana was a wonderful house in every way except one. But if it still existed, nothing on earth could make me set foot in it again. I truly believe it was haunted in a very real and frightening way. Most ghosts, when they appear, don't actually do much harm. They might scare people, but those people usually recover. Sometimes ghosts are even friendly. But whatever haunted the Villa Cascana was not friendly. If things had gone even a little differently, I doubt I would have survived my visit, just as Arthur Inglis didn't.

The house sat on a hill covered in oak trees, near Sestri di Levante on the Italian Riviera. It looked out over the sparkling blue sea, and behind it rose green forests of chestnut trees, which eventually gave way to dark pine woods at the hilltops. Around the villa, the gardens were bursting with spring flowers, filling the air with the scents of magnolia and roses, mixed with the fresh salt wind from the ocean. The cool, vaulted rooms were filled with this perfume.

The ground floor had a wide, columned porch—or loggia—around three sides, and the roof of this porch formed a balcony for the rooms on the first floor. A grand staircase made of gray marble led from the main hall up to the first-floor landing, where there were three rooms:

two large sitting rooms and an empty bedroom connected together. The bedroom wasn't being used, but the sitting rooms were.

From the landing, the staircase continued up to the second floor, where some more bedrooms were, including mine. Across the landing, a short flight of steps led to another small group of rooms, where Arthur Inglis had his bedroom and studio. My hosts, Jim Stanley and his wife, stayed in another wing of the house, where the servants also lived.

I arrived just in time for lunch on a bright, hot day in mid-May. After the long, sweaty walk up from the marina, I should have found the coolness of the house refreshing. But—and I can only offer my word on this—the moment I stepped inside, I felt something was wrong. This feeling was strong, although very vague. When I saw letters waiting for me in the hall, I immediately thought they must contain bad news. Yet when I opened them, I found only happy news—everyone wrote that they were well and doing fine. Still, my uneasiness didn't go away. Even in that cool, sweet-smelling house, something felt off.

I mention this because it might explain why, even though I usually sleep like a log, I slept very poorly on my first night at Villa Cascana. It might also explain why, when I finally did sleep—or dream—I had such a strange and vivid dream. Something entered my mind that had never been there before. But to be fair, I should add that a few things said during the day might have planted ideas in my head.

After lunch, Mrs. Stanley showed me around the house. She mentioned the empty bedroom on the first floor, which opened off the dining room where we had eaten.

"We left that bedroom empty," she said. "Jim and I have a lovely bedroom and dressing room in the other wing. If we used this room, we'd have to turn the dining room into a dressing room and eat downstairs. This way, we have our little apartment, Arthur has his in the other passage—and I remembered you once said you like being high up in a house. So we put you at the top."

For a moment, I felt a vague doubt—why explain all this unless there was something she wasn't saying? I couldn't help wondering if there was a reason they didn't use the empty room.

The second thing that might have influenced my dream happened at dinner. The conversation briefly turned to ghosts. Inglis declared firmly that anyone who believed in ghosts was a complete fool. After that, the subject was dropped. I don't remember anything else that could have suggested what happened later.

We all went to bed early. I yawned all the way upstairs, feeling terribly sleepy. My room was warm, so I threw open the windows. The moonlight poured in, and I listened to the nightingales singing in the garden. I undressed quickly and got into bed, but instead of falling asleep, I felt very wide awake. Still, I didn't mind. I was happy lying there, listening to the music of the night.

Maybe I fell asleep; maybe not. I thought I noticed the nightingales falling silent, and the moon sinking out of sight. I thought that if I was going to lie awake, I might as well read. I remembered I had left my book in the dining room downstairs. So I got out of bed, lit a candle, and went to fetch it.

I found the book on a side table in the dining room—but I also saw something else. The door to the empty bedroom was open, and a strange grayish light was spilling out.

I looked in.

The big four-poster bed stood right across from the door. And the weird light was coming from the bed—or more precisely, from what was on the bed.

It was crawling with giant caterpillars, each at least a foot long. They gave off a faint, ghostly glow, which lit up the whole room. These were not ordinary caterpillars. Instead of soft little feet, they had rows of crab-like pincers that clutched at whatever they touched as they dragged their bodies forward. Their color was a sickly yellow-gray, and their bodies were covered in lumps and bumps.

There were hundreds of them, writhing and crawling over each other, forming a horrible moving mound on the bed. Every now and then, one would slip off and fall to the floor with a soft, heavy thud. The concrete floor gave way under their pincer feet as if it were soft clay, and they would crawl back up onto the bed to rejoin the others.

They had no faces—just a sideways mouth that opened and closed as they breathed.

As I stood there staring, it felt like all the caterpillars suddenly noticed me. Every mouth turned toward me, and the next thing I knew, they started dropping off the bed one by one with soft, heavy thuds and wriggled across the floor toward me. For one frozen second, I couldn't move—then I bolted upstairs to my room, feeling the cold marble stairs under my bare feet as I ran.

I rushed into my bedroom, slammed the door shut behind me, and stood by my bed, wide awake now, sweating in terror. I could still hear the echo of the slammed door. Normally, if I had just been dreaming, the fear would have faded by now. But it didn't. If anything, it was worse. I felt completely awake—and completely sure that what I had seen was real.

I didn't dare lie down. Instead, I stood or sat up all night, certain that every tiny noise was one of those horrible creatures crawling toward me. I kept imagining their pincers biting into the floor and then easily tearing through the wood of my door. It felt like even steel wouldn't have kept them out.

But when morning finally came, the horror lifted. The gentle wind outside sounded friendly again, and the terror that had gripped me smoothed away. The dawn started colorless, then turned a soft grey, and finally exploded into a glowing sunrise across the sky.

At the villa, everyone had breakfast whenever and wherever they liked, so I didn't see anyone else until lunchtime. I ate breakfast alone on my balcony, then spent the morning writing letters. I even got to lunch a bit late, after the others had already started. When I sat down, I noticed a small cardboard pillbox placed between my knife and fork. Inglis spoke up right away.

"Take a look at that," he said. "You like natural history, right? I found it crawling on my bed last night. I have no idea what it is."

Before I even opened the box, I had a horrible feeling about what I would find. And sure enough, when I opened it, there it was—a small caterpillar, greyish-yellow with strange lumps and bumps all along its body. It moved quickly, scuttling around inside the box. Its feet weren't like a normal caterpillar's at all—they looked like tiny crab claws.

I quickly shut the lid again.

"I don't know what it is," I said. "But it doesn't look very healthy. What are you planning to do with it?"

"I'm going to keep it," Inglis said. "It's starting to spin a cocoon, and I want to see what kind of moth it turns into."

I opened the box again briefly and saw that, sure enough, the little thing was beginning to weave its cocoon.

"It has funny feet too," Inglis added. "They're just like crab pincers. What's Latin for crab? Oh, right—Cancer. Let's name it Cancer Inglisensis, just in case it's a new species."

Something clicked in my brain right then. His words somehow pulled together everything I had seen—or thought I had seen—the night before. The horror I'd felt watching the crawling creatures returned full force. Without thinking, I grabbed the pillbox and threw it out the open window.

Outside, there was a gravel path and a fountain. The box landed right in the fountain's basin.

Inglis laughed.

"So the ghost expert doesn't like real facts," he joked. "Poor little caterpillar!"

The conversation quickly moved on to other things, and I only mention all this in such detail because I want to be sure I've told everything that might explain what happened later. When I threw that box into the fountain, I admit I completely panicked. But can you blame me? That tiny caterpillar was exactly like the monsters I had seen covering the bed. And seeing it alive—real—didn't make the memory less frightening. It made it a hundred times worse.

After lunch, we spent a lazy couple of hours strolling around the garden or sitting under the loggia. Around four o'clock, Stanley and I decided to go swimming. We took the path that passed right by the fountain where I had thrown the pillbox.

The water was shallow and clear, and I could see the remains of the box at the bottom. The cardboard had fallen apart, leaving just some soggy scraps. In the center of the fountain stood a marble statue of a boy—an Italian Cupid—squirting water from a wineskin tucked under his arm.

And there, crawling up the leg of the statue, was the caterpillar.

As unbelievable as it sounds, it had survived the fall, crawled out of the wrecked box, and made its way up the statue. It waved back and forth, already starting to spin its cocoon.

As I stared at the caterpillar, it felt again like it noticed me. It broke free from the threads it had spun and started crawling quickly down the marble leg of the Cupid statue. Then, like a snake, it began swimming across the water toward me. I had never heard of a caterpillar being able to swim before, and it moved shockingly fast. In another second, it was climbing up the marble edge of the fountain basin.

Just then, Inglis joined me.

"Hey, it's old Cancer Inglisensis again," he said when he spotted it. "It's in quite a hurry."

We stood side by side on the path, and when the caterpillar got about a yard away, it stopped and waved around, like it couldn't decide which way to go. Then it made up its mind and crawled onto Inglis' shoe.

"I guess it likes me best," he said. "But I'm not sure I like it. And since it won't drown, I think—"

He shook it off his shoe onto the gravel and crushed it under his foot.

That afternoon, the air got heavier and heavier, and it was clear a sirocco wind from the south was blowing in. That night, I went to bed feeling very sleepy again, but underneath my drowsiness, I had an even stronger feeling than before—that something was wrong in the house, something dangerous.

Still, I fell asleep right away. I don't know how long I slept, but either I woke up or dreamed I woke up, feeling an urgent need to get up before it was too late. I lay there for a bit, fighting the fear, telling myself it was just nerves from the weather. But deep down, I knew every second I stayed in bed made the danger worse.

Finally, I couldn't resist anymore. I threw on my coat and trousers and stepped out onto the landing. Right away, I saw it was already too late.

The entire landing below me was crawling with caterpillars. The folding doors into the sitting-room were shut, but the caterpillars were squeezing through the cracks and oozing through the keyhole, stretching themselves out like strings to fit, then puffing back up on the other side. Some were crawling toward the passage that led to Inglis' rooms, and others had already reached the bottom of the staircase leading up to me. The whole landing was completely covered. I was trapped—and the terror I felt can't even be described.

Then, slowly, they all started moving toward Inglis' door. Like a horrible living tide, they slithered across the floor. I could see the first ones reaching his door, their pale, glowing bodies visible even in the dim light. Over and over, I tried to scream and warn him, but no sound would come out. I kept trying, terrified that if I made any noise, they would turn and come up toward me instead. They squeezed through the cracks in his door just like before, slipping inside one by one.

I stayed frozen where I was until the entire landing was empty again. Then, for the first time, I noticed the bitter cold of the marble floor under my bare feet. Out the window, I saw the first pale light of dawn breaking in the eastern sky.

Six months later, I ran into Mrs. Stanley at a country house in England. We talked about all sorts of things, until at last she said:

"I don't think I've seen you since I got that dreadful news about Arthur Inglis a month ago."

"I haven't heard," I said.

"No? He has cancer. The doctors say there's no hope—not even an operation could help. It's spread everywhere."

For the past six months, there hadn't been a day when I didn't think about what I had seen—or dreamed—at Villa Cascana.

"That's awful," I said. "And I can't help wondering—" she paused, "—whether he might have—"

"Caught it at the villa?" I asked.

She stared at me in total shock.

"Why did you say that?" she asked. "How could you know?"

Then she explained. A year earlier, someone had died of cancer in the unoccupied bedroom. Of course, she had gotten the best advice, and was told that everything would be perfectly safe as long as no one slept in that room. They had also disinfected it completely, painting and cleaning everything.

But still—

The Cat

A lot of people probably still remember that exhibition at the Royal Academy not too many years ago, the one that became known as Alingham's year. That was when Dick Alingham suddenly rose out of the crowd of struggling artists and landed right at the very top, gaining instant fame. He showed three portraits that year, each one a masterpiece, and together they completely outshined every other painting in the gallery. But no one cared much about the other paintings anyway—those three stole all the attention.

The way he became famous was as sudden as a shooting star flashing across the night sky, or like a hidden spring bursting out of dry rocks. Some said it was like a forgotten fairy godmother waving her wand and giving him a magical gift. But others, like Jim Merwick, had a different idea—one he explained in his paper On Certain Obscure Lesions of the Nerve Centers.

Dick Alingham, naturally, was thrilled, whether his success came from a fairy godmother or some strange illness (Merwick's paper was written after Dick's death). Dick once admitted to Merwick, who was still a struggling young doctor at the time, that he didn't really understand it himself.

"All I know," Dick said, "is that last fall, I went through two months of the worst depression you could imagine. Every day, I felt like my mind was about to snap. I would just sit here for hours, waiting for something inside me to break, and thinking that when it did, everything would be over. Yes, there was a reason—you know it."

He paused, poured himself a generous glass of whisky, filled it halfway with soda, and lit a cigarette. The reason didn't need to be explained: Merwick remembered perfectly well how the girl Dick had been engaged to dumped him very suddenly for a better match. The new man had everything—good looks, a title, and a fortune—and Lady Madingley, Dick's former fiancée, didn't seem to regret her choice at all. She was one of those rare, beautiful, cat-like women who are both graceful and dangerously charming.

"I don't need to talk about the cause," Dick went on. "But for two whole months, I honestly thought madness was the only ending. Then one night, while I was sitting here alone—as usual—something inside my head just snapped. I remember wondering, without even caring much, whether this was the madness I had feared or whether something worse had happened. But even while I wondered, I realized that I wasn't unhappy anymore."

He smiled, lost for a moment in his memory, and Merwick gave a small gesture to remind him he had an audience.

"Well?" Merwick said.

"It was the best thing that could have happened. I haven't been unhappy since. I've been completely, wildly happy instead. Some divine doctor, I guess, wiped away whatever was hurting inside my brain. God, how badly it hurt! Want a drink, by the way?"

"No thanks," said Merwick. "But what's all this got to do with your painting?"

"Everything. The moment I realized I was happy again, I also noticed that the world around me looked different. The colors were brighter, the shapes sharper. Before, everything had seemed dusty and faded, but now the lights had been turned on, and it was like I was seeing a brand new world. And right then, I knew I could paint it exactly as I saw it. Which," he added, smiling, "I've done."

There was something almost grand about the way he said this, and Merwick laughed.

"I wish something would snap in my head too, if it would make me see like that," he said. "But maybe not every 'snap' leads to something good."

"That's true. Also, I think things only snap after you've been through something truly awful, like I did. And believe me, I wouldn't go through that again even if it meant seeing the world like Titian."

"What did it feel like when it snapped?" asked Merwick.

Dick thought for a moment.

"You know when you get a package tied up with string and you can't find a knife?" he said. "So you burn the string by pulling it tight over a flame? Well, it was like that. It didn't hurt at all, just got weaker and weaker until it broke softly. Not very clear, I know—but that's exactly how it felt. It had been burning for two months, you see."

Then he turned away and rummaged through the papers scattered on his desk until he found an envelope with a small crown printed on it. He chuckled to himself as he picked it up.

"Give credit to Lady Madingley," said Dick, laughing, "for having nerves tougher than steel. She wrote to me yesterday asking if I would finish the portrait I started of her last year—and she said I could name my own price."

"I'd say you got pretty lucky," said Merwick. "I assume you didn't even bother replying?"

"Oh, I replied," said Dick. "Why not? I told her the price would be two thousand pounds, and that I was ready to start right away. She agreed and even sent me a cheque for a thousand today."

Merwick stared at him, completely shocked. "Are you out of your mind?" he asked.

"I hope not," said Dick calmly. "Though, to be fair, even doctors like you don't know exactly where sanity ends and madness begins."

Merwick stood up. "But don't you see what a huge risk you're taking?" he said. "Seeing her again, being around her while you paint—looking at her for hours! I saw her this afternoon, and honestly, she looked more like some creature than a real person. Won't it all come rushing back? Everything you felt before? It's too dangerous."

Dick shook his head firmly. "There's no danger at all," he said. "I feel absolutely nothing toward her now. Not even hatred. And honestly, if I hated her, that would be dangerous—it would mean she still mattered. But she doesn't. Thinking about her doesn't stir any feelings in me at all. And really, this kind of complete calm deserves a reward. I admire things on that level."

As he finished speaking, he drank the rest of his whisky and immediately poured himself another.

"That's your fourth," Merwick pointed out.

"Is it? I never keep track," Dick said with a grin. "Counting drinks seems petty. Besides, drinking doesn't affect me anymore."

"Then why do it?" asked Merwick.

"Because if I stop," Dick explained, "this incredible brightness—the vividness of color and sharpness of everything I see—fades a little."

"That can't be good for you," said the doctor.

Dick laughed. "Look at me carefully," he said, "and if you can honestly say I show any sign of drinking too much, I'll quit right now."

And honestly, it would have been hard to find anything wrong with him. Dick stood there for a moment, holding the glass in one hand and the bottle in the other. His body was steady; there wasn't the slightest tremor. His face was tanned and healthy, not bloated or thin. His skin was clear and firm. His eyes were bright too, without any puffiness or sagging around them. He looked like someone in top athletic shape—lean, quick, and full of energy. Even Merwick, trained as he was to notice the smallest signs of nervous trouble, had to admit there was no hint of it in Dick. His appearance and his behavior both seemed completely normal.

But Dick had always been unusual. His story just now—the deep sadness, the sudden "snap" that freed him from heartbreak—it was strange. His sudden leap from being a pretty average artist to a brilliant one was strange too. So maybe there was something strange happening now as well.

"Fine, I admit you show no sign of drinking too much," Merwick said. "But if I were treating you—and I'm not trying to get your business—I'd make you quit drinking and stay in bed for a month."

"Why on earth would you do that?" asked Dick.

"Because common sense says it's the smart thing to do," Merwick answered. "You went through a terrible emotional shock—anyone could see that from how badly you suffered. After a shock, you're supposed to take it slow, recover your strength. Instead, you're racing full-speed ahead, painting better than ever. I agree, it seems to be working, but—"

He stopped.

"But what's nonsense?" Dick asked, curious.

"You're the problem," said Merwick. "Professionally, I can't stand you because you seem to break a theory that I'm sure is true. I keep trying to explain it, but right now, I can't."

"What's the theory?" Dick asked.

"It's about how to treat shock. And also that if you want to do really good work, you should eat and drink very little and get lots of sleep. How much do you sleep, by the way?"

Dick thought for a second.

"Oh, I usually go to bed around three in the morning," he said. "I guess I sleep about four hours."

"And you live on whisky, eat like a prize goose, and could probably win a race tomorrow," Merwick said. "Go away—or maybe I should. Maybe you'll break down. That would make me feel better. But even if you don't, it's still really interesting."

In truth, Merwick found it more than just interesting. When he got home that night, he pulled a dusty book off his shelf and looked up a chapter called "Shock." It was a medical book about rare diseases and strange conditions of the nervous system. He had read it many times before because he specialized in unusual cases. But tonight, one paragraph grabbed his attention even more than usual.

It said:

"The nervous system can behave in ways that even the smartest doctors would never expect. There are real cases where people who couldn't move at all jumped out of bed if they heard a cry of 'Fire!' And sometimes, after a terrible emotional shock that causes deep depression, the brain goes into an overactive state. People might suddenly discover new talents or have an extreme burst of energy. They often need lots of food and alcohol to keep going. But sooner or later, they usually crash completely—whether their stomachs stop working, they have a mental breakdown, or they suddenly lose their minds."

But the weeks went by. London steamed under the hot July sun, and Dick Alingham kept working hard, painting brilliantly, and showing no signs of slowing down. Merwick secretly watched him closely and was completely baffled. Dick had promised that if Merwick ever spotted any sign of him drinking too much, he would quit. But there were no signs at all.

Meanwhile, Lady Madingley had come for several painting sessions. Merwick had warned Dick about the risks of seeing her again, but he had been wrong. Surprisingly, Dick and Lady Madingley had become good friends. And it was clear that Dick had no feelings for her anymore—he might as well have been painting a still life instead of a woman he once loved deeply.

One morning in mid-July, she was posing for him in his studio. Dick, who was usually cheerful while painting, was oddly quiet. He kept frowning at the canvas, chewing on the ends of his brushes, and frowning at her, too. Suddenly, he gave an impatient sigh.

"It's so close to looking like you," he said, "but it's not quite right. I keep making you look like you're listening to some boring hymn—one of those terrible ones in four sharps, written by some organist after a big meal. And that's not you at all!"

She laughed.

"You must be pretty clever to put all that into a painting," she said.

"I am," said Dick.

"Where do you see all that in me?"

Dick sighed again.

"In your eyes, of course," he said. "You show everything through your eyes. We talked about it a long time ago—you're a throwback to the animal world. Animals show everything through their eyes too."

"Oh? I thought dogs barked and cats scratched," she said with a smile.

"Sure, if it gets serious," Dick said. "But before that, it's all in the eyes. A happy dog, a jealous dog, a hungry one—you can tell just by looking at their eyes. Their mouths don't change much, and cats even less."

"You've often told me I'm like a cat," Lady Madingley said, totally calm.

"By Jove, yes," Dick agreed. "Maybe if I stared into a cat's eyes, it would help me figure out what's missing in the painting. Thanks for the idea!"

He set down his paint palette and went over to a side table with bottles, ice, and a soda siphon.

"No drink for you this hot morning?" he asked.

"No, thanks," she said. "Now, when will you give me my final sitting? You said you only needed one more."

Dick poured himself a drink.

"Well, I'm taking this down to the country," he said, nodding toward the painting. "I need to finish the background I told you about. If everything goes well, it'll take me three days. If not, maybe a week. Oh, I'm so excited about it! So how about a week from tomorrow?"

Lady Madingley pulled out a small jeweled notebook and made a note.

"And when I see it next," she teased, "will I find you've painted cat eyes instead of mine?"

Dick laughed.

"Oh, you won't even notice the difference," he said. "Funny, though—I've always hated cats. They actually make me feel faint. And yet you always remind me of one."

"You'll have to ask your friend Mr. Merwick about mysteries like that," she said with a smile.

The background of the painting was still just a rough idea—only a few bright purple and green patches near Lady Madingley's head. Dick could hardly wait to really get started. In his finished painting, he planned to show a green trellis covered almost completely by huge purple clematis flowers behind the tall figure on the narrow canvas. Above her would be a strip of soft summer sky, and below her feet, a small patch of grey-green grass. Everything else would be a bold pattern of green leaves and purple flowers.

To make this happen, Dick was heading to his little country house near Godalming. In the garden, he had built a simple outdoor studio—really just a shelter open to the north—right next to the trellis, which was now bursting with purple blooms.

He knew that with this background, Lady Madingley's striking beauty would stand out even more. Her wide grey hat, her shining grey dress, her yellow hair, and her pale eyes—sometimes blue, sometimes green or grey—would seem to glow. It was a project he was thrilled to finish. For anyone who creates, there's no joy greater than bringing an idea to life, and Dick's excitement only grew as he traveled to Godalming. Each flower and leaf he painted would make her seem even more alive, the way stars pop into view as the sky darkens at night.

His garden wasn't large, but it was neatly enclosed by old brick walls, and he had used the space cleverly. His small grassy yard—more a patch than a real lawn—was now mostly taken up by the studio. One side had a solid wooden wall, while the other two sides had trellises covered in climbing plants, with colorful fabrics hanging inside for decoration. In summer, Dick spent most of his days there, painting or relaxing. The ground, once grassy but now bare, was covered with Persian rugs. There were two tables, a bookcase full of his favorite books, and some wicker chairs. One corner was filled with gardening tools—a mower, a hose, a spade, and shears. Like many people who live intensely, Dick found peace in gardening. It gave his mind something simple and rewarding to focus on. Plants always responded to care, and even a little effort could lead to beautiful surprises. After a month away in London, he was eager to see what had changed in his garden.

Now the clematis was thanking him with more flowers than he could have hoped for, each one ready to become part of his painting.

That evening was hot but not stormy—the clear, gentle heat of summer. Dick had dinner alone in his shelter, using the golden sunset as his light. The sky slowly faded into deep velvet blue, but he stayed outside, sipping coffee and looking out across the garden toward a row of acacia trees that separated his property from the neighbor's. The trees, full and green, swayed gently in the warm air. Below them was a small raised strip of grass, and nearer were his flowerbeds, where sweet peas filled the air with their fragrance and the roses bloomed in shades of pink, copper, and deep red. The green trellis nearby was overflowing with purple clematis.

Dick wasn't really focused on anything—he was just soaking in the colors and scents—when something caught his eye. A dark shape moved among the roses, and suddenly two glowing eyes stared right at him. He jumped up, startled, but the creature—a cat—wasn't scared at all. It calmly walked closer, its back arched for petting and its tail stiff like a stick. As it came nearer, Dick felt that familiar sickly weakness he often got around cats. He clapped his hands and stamped his feet to scare it away. The cat turned quickly, darted up the garden wall like a shadow, and disappeared. But the magic of the evening was broken, and Dick went inside.

The next morning was crystal clear. A soft north breeze blew, and the bright, golden sunlight made the garden shine like a scene from Greece. Dick had slept deeply and peacefully, and the strange moment with the cat was already forgotten. He set up his canvas facing the trellis, feeling a wave of excitement. In the full light of morning, the garden was even more dazzling than it had been at sunset. Life hadn't been easy for him lately—especially after everything with Lady Madingley—but he reminded himself that with a love for painting and gardening, a person could still build a happy life.

After breakfast, he jumped straight into his work. His model—the blooming clematis—was ready, and he felt a surge of joy as he began sketching the big shapes of leaves and flowers.

Purple and green, green and purple—could anything be more thrilling? Dick was completely caught up in the work, and he immediately knew he had made the right choice. The bold colors would make Lady Madingley's figure pop right off the canvas. The small patch of sky above her head and the grass below her feet would anchor her perfectly. Every brushstroke felt confident and right, bringing the whole scene to life.

Finally, he stopped, breathless and slightly dizzy, as if he had traveled far and only just returned. He had been working for about three hours—his servant was already setting the lunch table—but to him it felt like no time at all. The progress he had made was incredible, and he stood there, studying his painting with deep satisfaction.

Then his eyes wandered from the bright canvas back to the real garden, sparkling in the sun. And there, just a few feet away near the sweet peas, sat a large grey cat, perfectly still, watching him.

Normally, seeing a cat made Dick feel sick and faint, but at that moment, as he and the cat stared at each other, he didn't feel any of that. He figured it must be because he was outside in the fresh air instead of trapped indoors. Still, he remembered that the cat from the night before had made him feel faint even out here—but he didn't think much about it now. What grabbed his attention was that the look in this cat's eyes was exactly what had been missing in his painting of Lady Madingley.

Carefully, so he wouldn't scare it away, Dick reached for his palette and, in a few quick, instinctive brushstrokes, captured the look he needed in a blank corner of the canvas. Even in the bright sunlight, the cat's eyes seemed to glow from within and outside at the same time. That was exactly how Lady Madingley's eyes had seemed. He realized he would have to paint the color very lightly over white to get the same effect.

For about five minutes, he worked quietly, laying down thin layers of color. Then he stepped back and studied what he had painted. It was just what he wanted. He turned to thank the cat for being such a good model—but it had vanished. Still, Dick wasn't disappointed. He hated cats anyway, and this one had given him exactly what he needed.

The gift it left him—captured forever on the canvas—was more valuable than the cat's sudden disappearance. This was going to be the best portrait he had ever made: a woman, real and alive, with her soul shining through her eyes, surrounded by the wildness of summer.

All day, Dick's vision stayed incredibly sharp, though by sunset he had finished off a whole bottle of whisky. For the first time, he noticed two strange feelings: first, a heavy, uncomfortable sensation in his body, like he had drunk too much; second, an unwelcome stirring of the old heartbreak he thought he had left behind—the pain from when Lady Madingley had tossed him aside. Neither feeling was very strong, but both unsettled him.

By evening, the weather had turned. Thick clouds rolled in, and the clean heat of summer gave way to a sticky, stormy heaviness. A few heavy raindrops warned him that a storm was coming, so Dick pulled his easel into shelter and decided to have dinner indoors. He preferred to eat alone when working, to avoid distractions.

After dinner, Dick settled into his sitting-room for a quiet night. The tray had been brought in, and he planned to stay undisturbed until bedtime. Outside, the storm grumbled in the distance, moving closer. Every so often, thunder growled in the sky, and any minute, it might burst overhead.

Dick tried to read, but his thoughts kept drifting. That old heartbreak, which he had thought dead and buried, stirred up sharply again. His head felt heavy too—maybe from the storm, maybe from the alcohol. Deciding he'd be better off sleeping it off, he closed his book and walked toward the window to shut it for the night.

But halfway there, he froze. On the sofa by the window sat a large grey cat with glowing yellow eyes. In its mouth, it held a young thrush, still alive.

A wave of horror hit him. The old sick feeling returned stronger than ever, and he felt a sickening terror at the sight of the cat so pleased with the suffering of its prey. It wasn't eating the bird yet—just savoring its helplessness. Worse still, the cat's eyes were a twisted, horrifying match to the eyes he had painted in Lady Madingley's portrait.

For a moment, Dick was paralyzed. Then, unable to stand it any longer, he threw the glass he was holding at the cat. He missed. The cat paused, glaring at him with pure hatred, then sprang through the open window and disappeared.

Dick slammed the window shut so hard that it shook the room. He frantically searched the sofa and floor for the bird, thinking maybe it had been dropped. A couple of times, he thought he heard a faint flutter, but he found nothing.

Feeling rattled, Dick poured himself one last drink to "steady" his nerves, as he told himself. Outside, the thunder had stopped, but heavy rain still poured down. Then, through the sound of the rain, he heard something else: the soft mewing of a cat, the kind of pitiful cry of a pet wanting to be let inside.

The blind was down, but Dick couldn't resist taking a peek. On the windowsill, soaked by the rain but looking strangely dry, sat the grey cat again. When it saw him, it hissed, scratched angrily at the glass, and vanished into the night.

Lady Madingley... My God, how he had loved her! Even after everything—after how cruelly she had thrown him aside—he realized with a jolt that he still wanted her, with a passion as strong as ever. Was it all starting again? Had that nightmare he thought he had escaped come back to haunt him? It had to be the cat's fault—the cat's eyes had brought it all rushing back.

But now, his old desire was mixed with a strange dullness in his mind, a heavy fog he couldn't explain. For months, he had drunk heavily and still stayed sharp at night, enjoying the freedom and the rush of creativity. Tonight, though, he stumbled across the room, clumsy and confused.

The pale morning light woke him. Still groggy, he got out of bed, feeling a strong, silent urge pulling at him. The storm had passed, and a bright morning star glowed in the early sky. The room looked strange, unfamiliar. So did the way he felt—hazy and disconnected, like he was separated from the world around him. Only one thought stayed clear: he had to finish the portrait. Everything else—life, rules, chance—meant nothing now.

Two hours later, his servant came to call him for breakfast and found Dick's room empty. Thinking he had gone outside to enjoy the fine weather, the man went out to set breakfast in the garden shelter.

There, in front of the trellis, was the portrait, dragged roughly back into place. But it was scratched and torn, as if some furious animal—or maybe a man—had attacked it with claws.

And lying in front of the ruined painting was Dick Alingham, perfectly still. His throat was horribly torn, as if by claws or nails. His hands were covered in paint, and his nails were packed with it.

The Bus-Conductor

My friend Hugh Grainger and I had just come back from a two-day trip to the countryside. We had been staying at a house known for its creepy reputation—people said it was haunted by especially frightening and aggressive ghosts. The house looked exactly like you'd expect a haunted house to look: old, Jacobean-style, with oak-paneled walls, long dark hallways, and high, vaulted rooms. It stood all by itself, surrounded by a thick forest of dark pine trees that seemed to whisper and mutter whenever the wind blew.

During our stay, a strong southwest storm had been raging, with pounding rain and fierce winds. Day and night, strange noises echoed through the chimneys, the trees seemed full of whispering voices, and the windows rattled and tapped as if someone—or something—was trying to get in. Given all that, you would have thought something supernatural would show up. But absolutely nothing happened.

I have to admit, though, that my nerves were ready to invent anything. I was scared the entire time, lying awake for hours both nights, terrified of the dark, yet just as scared of what I might see if I lit a candle.

The night after we got back to the city, Hugh came over for dinner. Naturally, our conversation soon turned back to our ghost-hunting adventure.

"I really don't know why you go looking for ghosts," Hugh said. "You were shaking with fear the whole time. Your teeth were chattering, and your eyes looked ready to pop out of your head. Do you actually like being scared?"

Hugh is smart most of the time, but sometimes he completely misses the point—this was one of those times.

"Of course I like being scared," I said. "I want to feel my skin crawl and my hair stand on end. Fear is the most exciting feeling. When you're really afraid, you forget everything else."

"Well, the fact that neither of us saw anything proves what I've always believed," he said.

"And what's that?" I asked.

"That ghosts are completely real, not just something people imagine. Your state of mind doesn't matter. Nor do creepy houses or scary settings. If ghosts were only in your head, Osburton would have been the perfect place to imagine one, and you, with your nerves on edge, would have been the perfect person to see one. But you didn't."

Hugh got up and lit a cigarette. He's a big guy—tall and broad—and as I watched him, I almost made a joke about how there had been a time when Hugh himself was a wreck, a nervous mess. Strangely, he brought it up himself for the first time.

"You might say I was the wrong man to go ghost-hunting, considering how messed up I used to be," he said. "But I wasn't. You've never seen a ghost, even though you get scared so easily. I have. And even though I'm back to normal now, what I saw nearly destroyed me."

He sat back down.

"I'm sure you remember when I completely fell apart," he said. "Now that I feel normal again, I think I can finally talk about it. Before, I couldn't even bring it up. It was too much. Yet what I saw wasn't even threatening—it was actually a helpful, friendly ghost. But it came from the mysterious side of life, from the unknown, and that alone was enough to shake me."

He paused a moment, then continued.

"First, let me quickly explain how I think ghost-seeing works. It's easier to understand if I describe it with a picture in your mind. Imagine this: all of us are standing behind a sheet of cardboard that's constantly moving and spinning. In this sheet is a tiny hole, and we can only look through that tiny hole to the other side. Now, imagine there's another sheet of cardboard right next to it, also spinning and moving on its own. It has a hole too.

When by chance these two little holes line up, we can see through both sheets at once—and that's when we catch a glimpse of the spiritual world. Most people live their whole lives without those holes ever lining up. But at the moment of death, the holes stay lined up forever. That's how we 'cross over.'

Now, in some people, the holes are bigger, and they line up more often. Those are the mediums and clairvoyants. But for someone like me, who has no special powers, the holes almost never match. I had always assumed I would never see anything supernatural. But once—just once—the holes lined up. And it completely wrecked me."

I had heard ideas like this before. Hugh explained it in a colorful way, but honestly, there was nothing especially convincing about it. Maybe he was right—or maybe he wasn't.

"I hope your ghost story is more original than your theory," I said, trying to get him to the point.

"I think it is. You can be the judge," Hugh answered.

I added more coal to the fire and stirred it up. I've always thought Hugh had a real gift for storytelling—he has that sense of drama that's so important when telling a good story. I've even joked before that he should make it his career: sit by the fountain at Piccadilly Circus and tell stories for money like an old storyteller from the Arabian Nights.

Most people don't have the patience for long stories, but I love them, and Hugh is the perfect kind of storyteller for someone like me. His theories and comparisons I could do without—but when he tells about things that really happened, I like him to take his time.

"Take it slow, please," I said. "Being brief might be smart, but it ruins a good story. I want to know everything—where you were, what time it was, what you had for lunch, where you had dinner, all of it."

Hugh started:

"It happened on June 24th, about a year and a half ago. I had rented out my own flat and came up from the country to stay with you for a week. We had dinner alone here that night—"

I couldn't help interrupting.

"Wait—you saw the ghost here?" I asked. "In this little box of a house, on a normal street?"

"I was inside the house when I saw it," he said.

I kept quiet but hugged myself in excitement.

"We had dinner alone here on Graeme Street," he continued. "After dinner, I went out to a party, and you stayed home. I remember your man didn't serve dinner, and when I asked about him, you told me he was sick—and you changed the subject pretty quickly. When I left, you gave me your spare key. When I came back, you had already gone to bed, but there were a few letters for me that needed answering. So I sat down, wrote the replies, and mailed them at the box across the street. I guess it was pretty late by the time I headed upstairs.

"You had given me the front room on the third floor, the one overlooking the street—the room you usually sleep in yourself, I think. It was a hot night. Earlier, when I went to the party, the moon was out, but when I got back, the whole sky was covered in clouds, and it felt like we might get a thunderstorm before morning.

"I was tired and didn't notice until after I got into bed that only one window was open. It felt stuffy, but I didn't bother getting up to open the other one. I just went to sleep.

"I don't know what time I woke up, but it wasn't morning yet—there wasn't even the first hint of dawn. And I don't think I've ever noticed such complete silence before. No footsteps, no carriages, nothing. It was as if the whole world had gone still.

"But I wasn't sleepy anymore. Even though I couldn't have slept more than an hour or two, I felt wide awake. Now, it seemed easy enough to get out of bed, so I pulled up the blind, opened the other window, and leaned out. I was desperate for some air. Even outside, the air felt heavy and close. Normally, I'm not very sensitive to weather, but right then I felt this terrible creepiness. I tried to shake it off by reasoning with myself, but it didn't help. It had been a nice day, and tomorrow promised to be just as good, but I still felt this strange fear, and terribly alone.

"Then I heard something—far off at first—the slow clop of horses' hooves. A carriage or something was coming up the street, but instead of feeling less alone because of it, the feeling of dread only got worse. In a way I couldn't explain, I knew that whatever was coming had something to do with the fear I was feeling.

"Soon, it came into view. At first, I couldn't make out what it was. But then I saw the horses—both black, with long tails—and realized they were pulling something made of glass with a black frame. It was a hearse.

"But it was empty."

"It was coming up our side of the street and stopped right in front of your house.

"Then I had a thought. At dinner, you mentioned your servant was sick and didn't really want to talk about it. I figured maybe he had died, and for some reason—maybe because you didn't want me to know—you were having the body taken away at night. That thought came and went quickly, and I didn't even stop to think how unlikely that really was before the next thing happened.

"I was still leaning out of the window and noticed how strange it was that I could see everything so clearly. There was a moon behind the clouds, but it still seemed brighter than it should have been. I could see all the details of the hearse and the horses. There was only one person with it—the driver—and the rest of the street was totally empty. I looked closer at him. I could see every part of his outfit, but because I was looking down from the third floor, I couldn't see his face right away. He was wearing gray pants, brown boots, a black coat buttoned up, and a straw hat. There was a strap over his shoulder, like he was carrying a small bag. From how he looked, what would you have guessed he was?"

"A bus conductor," I said immediately.

"Exactly. That's what I thought too. Then, while I was still thinking that, he looked straight up at me. His face was long and thin, and there was a mole with dark hair on his left cheek. I saw it all so clearly, like it was daylight and I was standing right in front of him. But even with how strange that was, I didn't have time to question why a hearse driver would be dressed like that.

"Then he tipped his hat and pointed his thumb behind him.

"'Just room for one inside, sir,' he said.

"There was something so creepy and wrong about the way he said it that I quickly pulled my head inside, dropped the blind, and turned on the light to check the time. My watch said it was 11:30.

"That's when I started to really question what I had just seen. I turned off the light and got back into bed, thinking it over. We had eaten dinner, I went to a party, came back, wrote some letters, went to bed, and slept. So how could it still be 11:30? Or what kind of 11:30 was that?

"Then I figured maybe my watch had stopped. But it hadn't—I could hear it ticking.

"Everything outside was silent again. I kept waiting to hear quiet footsteps on the stairs, like someone was carrying something heavy. But there was nothing. The street was quiet too, even though the hearse was supposedly still there. Minutes went by, and the light started to change. Dawn was coming. But if it was really morning, why hadn't the hearse left?

"I finally got up, still feeling creeped out, and went to the window. I pulled the blind back. The sky was lit with that soft silver glow of early morning. But the hearse was gone.

"I looked at my watch again. It was 4:15. But I swear, it didn't feel like more than half an hour had passed since I saw it say 11:30.

"Then I felt this weird double feeling—like I was standing in the present but also still inside that moment with the hearse. It was morning now, but the man had spoken to me just a little while ago, and it had been nighttime. Who was he? Where had he come from? And what kind of 11:30 had I actually experienced?

"I told myself it was just a dream. But if you asked me whether I believed that, I'd have to say no.

"Your servant didn't come to breakfast the next morning, and I didn't see him before I left later that day. I think if I had, I might have told you everything. But there was still a small chance that what I saw had been real. Maybe there had actually been a hearse, and I'd fallen asleep before seeing it leave. So I said nothing."

The way he told the story was calm and plain, which somehow made it even more disturbing. There were no haunted mansions or howling trees—just a normal house and a normal street. That made it worse. Still, I wasn't sure.

"Don't tell me it was all a dream," I said.

"I don't know if it was," he said. "All I know is, I felt completely awake. But the rest of the story is... strange."

"I left the city that afternoon," he continued. "But I couldn't get that night out of my mind. It stayed with me like I was still waiting for something to happen—like a clock had chimed but never finished the hour.

"A month later, I came back to London for just one day. I arrived at Victoria Station around eleven and took the Underground to Sloane Square. It was a blazing hot morning, and I planned to catch a bus on King's Road to your place. There was a bus already there when I came out of the station. The top was full, and the inside looked full too. As I got closer, the conductor stepped out onto the steps—just a few feet away.

"He was wearing the same clothes: gray pants, brown boots, a buttoned-up black coat, a straw hat, and the same strap over his shoulder with the ticket machine. I saw his face—it was him. Same mole. Same man.

"And again, he looked at me, tipped his hat, and said, 'Just room for one inside, sir.'

"At that moment, I panicked. I waved my arms and yelled, 'No, no!' But I wasn't even in the present anymore—I was back in that other moment, looking out your window before dawn. I realized that my view into the spirit world had opened again, and what I saw back then was coming true now. I felt frozen, like something bigger than me was happening, something I couldn't stop or understand. I stood there shaking.

"The bus pulled away. I looked across the street at the post office. The clock in the window told me exactly what I expected.

"You probably know the rest," Hugh said. "You remember what happened near Sloane Square at the end of July that year.

"The bus pulled into the street to go around a van. Just then, a large car came speeding down King's Road. It crashed right into the side of the bus, like a drill going into wood."

He paused.

"And that's my story," he said.

The Man Who Went Too Far

The quiet village of St. Faith's rests in a small valley surrounded by forested hills, on the north side of the Fawn River in Hampshire. The houses are grouped closely around an old grey church, almost as if they're trying to stay safe—maybe from the fairies, trolls, or other strange creatures that some people still believe hide deep in the New Forest.

If you step outside the village and stay off the main road to Brockenhurst, you could wander for hours on a warm summer afternoon without spotting another house—or even another person. You might see a few scruffy wild ponies glance up from grazing, catch a flash of a rabbit's white tail as it darts into the grass, or notice a snake slip quietly into a patch of heather. Birds will be rustling and calling from the bushes, but chances are you won't see anyone else the whole time.

Still, it doesn't feel lonely. In summer, sunlight dances with butterflies, and the air is filled with the quiet music of the woods. The wind whispers in the birch trees and sighs through the pines. Bees hum as they work among the heather. Birds sing high in the trees. And the river laughs softly as it runs over stones, swirls in pools, and curves around bends, making it feel like nature is full of life and company.

But strangely, even with all this beauty and peace, the people of St. Faith's don't like to go into the forest after dark. You'd think the fresh air and open spaces would bring comfort, but something about the forest at night makes people uneasy. Though it's hard to get a clear story from the villagers, many believe you never know what—or who—you might meet in the woods after sunset. One tale that does get told is about a huge, creepy goat that's been seen leaping around the woods like something out of a nightmare. And that may be connected to the story I'm about to tell. The villagers know it well. Everyone remembers the young artist who died not too long ago. He was handsome and had a bright, uplifting presence that made people smile. They say his ghost still walks by the river and through the woods he loved so much. Most of all, it haunts the house at the far edge of the village—the one where he lived—and the garden where he was killed. I think that's when people really started to fear the forest.

This story comes from what the villagers have told me, but also from my friend Darcy, who knew the young man closely.

It was one of those perfect midsummer days, and as evening came, the light became even more beautiful—clear and glowing, like a dream. To the west of the village, the tall beech trees stretched toward the open moors, casting soft shadows over the red rooftops. But the church spire still caught the orange light of the setting sun, standing out against the sky. The Fawn River below reflected the sky's deep blue, winding lazily along the edge of the woods. A small wooden bridge crossed it near the garden of the last house in the village, connecting to the forest through a little gate made of wicker. Past the woods, the river glowed red and gold in the sunset before disappearing into the distance.

The house at the edge of the village still sat in sunlight. Its lawn ran down to the river, lined with flowerbeds bursting with color. A brick pergola ran through the middle of the garden, covered in climbing roses and purple clematis. A hammock was strung between two of its pillars, and someone was lying in it, wearing a shirt with the sleeves rolled up.

This house was far from the other homes in the village. The only way to reach it from the main road was by a footpath through two fields full of sweet-smelling hay. The house itself was small—just two stories high—and its walls were almost hidden under blooming roses. Along the garden front was a narrow stone terrace, shaded by a cloth awning. On the terrace, a quiet young servant was setting the dinner table. He worked quickly and neatly, then went into the house and came back with a large bath towel. He walked to the hammock and said,

"It's almost eight, sir."

"Has Mr. Darcy arrived yet?" asked the man in the hammock.

"No, sir."

"Well, if I'm not back by the time he comes, tell him I've gone for a swim before dinner."

The servant went back into the house, and after a few moments, Frank Halton sat up and climbed out of the hammock onto the grass. He was average in height and slim, but the way he moved—smooth and confident—made him seem stronger than he looked. Even getting out of the hammock looked graceful, not clumsy. His skin was dark from spending so much time outside in the sun and wind, though his dark hair and eyes suggested he might also have southern roots. His head was small, and his face was almost too perfect to be real—so smooth and youthful that you might think he was still a teenager. But there was a deeper look in his eyes, something that only comes with experience, that made you pause. You might start to wonder how old he really was, but then you'd probably stop thinking about it altogether and just admire how full of life he seemed.

He was dressed for the warm weather—just an open-neck shirt and light flannel pants. His thick, curly hair was uncovered as he strolled down to the riverbank. For a while, everything was quiet. Then there was a splash, and a moment later, a joyful shout as he swam against the current, water foaming around his neck. After swimming for a few minutes, he turned onto his back, arms spread wide, and floated with the stream, letting it carry him. His eyes were closed, and his lips moved softly as he spoke to himself.

"I'm part of it," he murmured. "The river and I are one. Its coolness, its splash—that's me. Even the plants under the surface are part of me. My strength, my body—it's all the river's. We're the same, sweet Fawn."

Fifteen minutes later, he came walking up from the river again, dressed like before. His wet hair had already begun to curl and dry. He stopped for a moment, smiling at the water like someone smiling at an old friend, then turned toward the house. At that same moment, his servant stepped out onto the terrace, followed by a man in his late thirties. Frank and the visitor saw each other across the garden, and both walked quickly until they met near a curve in the path, surrounded by the scent of blooming flowers.

"My dear Darcy," Frank said cheerfully, "I'm so glad you're here!"

But Darcy looked shocked.

"Frank?" he said in disbelief.

"That's me," Frank laughed. "What's wrong?"

Darcy grabbed his hand.

"What happened to you?" he asked. "You look like a kid again."

"I have a lot to explain," Frank said. "Stuff you might not believe, but I'll prove it—"

He stopped suddenly and held up a hand.

"Wait, listen… That's my nightingale," he whispered.

The happy look on his face disappeared. His expression turned soft and amazed, like someone hearing the voice of someone they love. His mouth opened slightly, showing a line of white teeth, and his eyes stared into the distance, as if he was seeing something no one else could. Then, the bird fell silent.

"Yes, there's so much to tell you," Frank said again. "But really, it's great to see you. You look a bit pale and tired, though—not surprising after that fever. And don't argue—you're staying here until you're completely better. Two full months at least."

"I don't think I can stay that long."

Frank looped his arm through Darcy's and guided him down the lawn.

"Don't be silly. I'll let you know when I'm tired of you. But remember, when we shared a studio, we never annoyed each other. Anyway, we shouldn't talk about leaving when you just got here. Let's take a quick walk by the river before dinner."

Darcy pulled out his cigarette case and offered it.

Frank laughed. "No thanks. Funny—I guess I used to smoke, didn't I? Seems strange now."

"You quit?"

"I suppose I did. I just don't anymore. It's like eating meat—I wouldn't even think of it."

"So you've gone vegetarian?"

"Vegetarian?" Frank smiled. "Do I look like I'm suffering?"

He paused at the riverbank and whistled softly. A moorhen flew across the water and walked up the bank. Frank gently picked it up and stroked its head as it rested against his shirt.

"And is your house still safe among the reeds?" he asked softly. "Is your partner doing well? Are your neighbors still around? Off you go now," he said, tossing the bird into the air.

"That bird's unusually tame," Darcy said, still surprised.

"It is," Frank replied, watching it fly away.

At dinner, Frank mostly spent time catching up on Darcy's life. In the six years they hadn't seen each other, Darcy had achieved a lot. He had become a well-known portrait artist, with a growing reputation. His time had been packed with work and success. A few months ago, though, he had gotten very sick with typhoid, and that illness was what brought him to this quiet village to rest and recover.

"You've really done well," Frank said. "I always knew you would. You're an A.R.A. now, and there's more ahead. You're probably rich too. But tell me—have you been happy? That's what really matters. And what have you learned? I don't mean in art. Even I could've done well in that."

Darcy laughed. "Done well? Frank, everything I've learned in the last six years, you already knew back when we were kids. Your old paintings are selling for huge amounts. Don't you paint anymore?"

Frank shook his head. "No. I'm too busy now."

"Doing what? Seriously—people keep asking me, and I don't know what to say."

"Doing? I guess you could say I've been doing nothing," Frank said.

Darcy looked at Frank's bright, youthful face.

"Well, whatever you've been doing, it's clearly working," he replied. "Now tell me—do you read or study? I remember you once said that artists would really benefit from studying one person's face for a whole year without even drawing it. Is that what you've been doing?"

Frank shook his head.

"No, I really meant it. I've been doing absolutely nothing. And yet, I've never felt more occupied in my life. Just look at me—don't you think I've changed?"

"You're two years younger than I am," Darcy said. "That makes you thirty-five. But if I didn't know you, I'd think you were only twenty. Was it really worth spending six years of your life just to look younger? You sound like a rich woman chasing eternal youth."

Frank burst out laughing.

"That's a first—I've never been compared to one of them before," he said. "But no, that's not what I've been trying to do. I don't really focus on looking younger—it just happened. Sure, I look young again, but more than that, I feel young."

Darcy turned his chair to face him more directly.

"Is that what you've been trying to achieve?" he asked.

"Well, part of it, yes. Think about what it means to be young. It's not just age—it's about growing. Your body, your mind, your spirit—they're all full of energy and becoming stronger. But most people, once they hit their peak, slowly start to fade. They don't notice it, but it happens. Their bodies weaken, their ideas get stuck, even their creativity dulls. You're not as sharp as you used to be. But me—I'm just starting to reach my peak. Just wait. You'll see."

Above them, the stars had started to shine in the darkening sky. In the east, behind the shadowy outline of the village, the sky was turning pale as the moon began to rise. White moths drifted through the garden, and the quiet of night settled in like soft footsteps.

Frank suddenly stood.

"This is the perfect moment," he said quietly. "Right now, more than ever, I feel the power of life all around me. It's so strong I feel like I'm surrounded by it. Just be still for a second."

He stepped to the edge of the terrace, stretched out his arms, and stood in silence. Darcy heard him breathe in deeply, hold it, and slowly breathe out. He did it again and again, six or seven times, before turning back to the light.

"You might think this sounds crazy," Frank said, "but if you want to hear the most honest thing I've ever said, I'll tell you about myself. Let's go out into the garden, if it's not too damp. I've never told anyone this before, but I feel like telling you now. It's been a while since I even tried to put it into words."

They walked into the quiet, flower-scented garden and sat in the pergola.

"Remember years ago, when we used to talk about how people didn't seem to feel joy anymore?" Frank began. "We figured there were lots of reasons for that—some good, some bad. Some good values, like self-control, compassion, and the desire to help others, are important. But they can go too far. You get people giving up happiness for no real reason, punishing themselves, or becoming cold and emotionless. Then there's something even worse—something that hurt this country long ago and still affects us now: Puritanism. It was like a sickness. Those people thought fun, laughter, and joy were sinful. That belief was harsh and wrong. Just look around—the most common thing you see is a gloomy face. That says everything."

He leaned back a little, relaxed.

"I've always believed that happiness is what we're meant for. Joy is the most powerful gift we can have. That's why I left London and gave up what little career I had. I wanted to chase joy with everything I had—to really be happy. But I couldn't find it in the city. There were too many distractions, too much pain. So I walked away—or maybe moved forward—and turned to nature. The trees, the birds, the animals… they all just want to be happy. They don't care about laws or rules like people do. I wanted joy straight from the source, untouched and real. I don't think humans really have it anymore. We've lost it."

Darcy looked over at him.

"But animals and birds—what makes them happy? Isn't it mostly just food and mating?"

Frank smiled in the quiet.

"Don't worry—I didn't become someone who just chases pleasure," he said. "That would be a huge mistake. People like that drag their misery around with them, even while they chase after fun. No, I wasn't that foolish. Think about it—why does a puppy chase its tail? Why do cats wander around at night, excited and alive?"

He paused, thoughtful.

"So I came here to the New Forest and just sat down. I watched. That was the hardest part at first—just sitting still, not getting bored, not getting restless. I had to be completely open and aware. For a while, nothing much changed. It was slow at the start."

"Nothing happened?" Darcy asked, raising an eyebrow. His voice held that usual doubt that shows up when someone hears something that feels strange or unfamiliar.

Frank, who used to be known for his quick temper but also his warm heart, didn't look upset at all. Darcy was already thinking of apologizing, but Frank just laughed—genuinely, with no sign of offense.

"Oh, a few years ago I would've taken offense at that," Frank said. "But thankfully, getting offended is one of the things I've let go of. I definitely want you to believe me—and I think you will—but the fact that you don't right now doesn't really bother me."

"Your time alone has made you a bit... strange," Darcy said, still holding on to his usual practical mindset.

"No," Frank replied, "it's made me more human. Maybe even less like a wild animal."

He paused, then continued, "My first goal was to search for happiness. I wanted it more than anything. So I focused completely on nature. Maybe that sounds selfish, but the result has been anything but. Happiness spreads fast—it's more contagious than any disease. So I sat still. I avoided anything sad and kept my eyes on joyful things. Slowly, little by little, the joy around me began to sink in. That trickle turned into a stream, and now, my friend, if I could transfer even half of the happiness that runs through me into you, you'd drop everything—your work, your art—and just live. When the body dies, it returns to the earth, becoming part of trees and flowers. What I've been trying to do is let my soul return before death."

While Frank spoke, the servant quietly brought drinks and a lamp into the pergola. As the soft light lit Frank's face, Darcy couldn't help but notice something strange—it was glowing. His skin looked lit from within, his dark eyes sparkled, and there was a peaceful, almost childlike smile on his face. Darcy felt a strange energy rising in him—excitement, even joy.

"Keep going," he said. "I can tell you're speaking honestly. Maybe you are a little crazy, but I don't think it matters."

Frank chuckled. "Crazy? Maybe. But I think it's actually the opposite—I think I've finally become sane. Still, who cares what we call it? Names aren't important. God doesn't label the things He gives us. He just hands them over, the same way He let Adam name the animals."

"By studying only joyful things," Frank went on, "I found joy. But I also discovered something else—something I wasn't even looking for. I'll try to explain it, though it's hard to put into words.

"About three years ago, I was sitting in a spot I'll show you tomorrow. It's by the river, in a green patch with sunlight and shade, and there are reeds growing along the water. I wasn't doing anything—just sitting, watching, listening. Then I heard a sound, soft and clear, like a flute playing a strange tune that never ended. At first, I thought it was someone on the road, maybe a country boy playing an instrument. I didn't pay much attention. But the melody kept going, changing every few moments. It never repeated but kept building and growing, one high point after another. Finally, I realized something that made me stop breathing—it wasn't coming from just one place. The sound came from the reeds, the sky, the trees. It was everywhere. It was the sound of life itself. The Greeks would've said it was Pan playing his pipes. It was the voice of nature. It was the music of the world."

Darcy leaned in, completely absorbed, even though a question was forming in his mind. Frank continued.

"I was terrified at first—like the kind of fear you feel in a nightmare, when you're helpless. I covered my ears and ran back to the house, shaking and out of breath. At the time, all I had been looking for was joy, but since I found it in nature, something else had started to happen. Life itself—nature, or God, whatever you want to call it—had touched me. It was like a tiny, invisible thread of pure life had brushed across my face. Once I calmed down, I saw that. So I went back, humbly, to the same spot. But it took six months before I heard that music again."

"Why did it take that long?" Darcy asked.

"Because I got scared," Frank said. "I panicked, I resisted, and worst of all—I let fear in. I truly believe that nothing harms the body more than fear, and nothing closes the soul off more completely. I was afraid of the one real thing in the world—life itself. So it pulled back."

"And after six months?"

"One beautiful morning, I heard the music again. That time, I wasn't afraid. Since then, it's been happening more often. The music comes clearer, louder. I can now bring myself into a state where I almost always hear it. And it's never the same song—it's always something new, deeper, fuller than before."

"What do you mean by 'a state'?" Darcy asked.

"I can't fully explain it," Frank said. "But I can show you physically what it's like."

He sat up tall, then slowly leaned back, letting his arms fall open and his head rest gently.

"That," he said, "is what it feels like inside. Not forced—just relaxed, open, ready to receive. That's what you need to do with your soul."

Then he straightened up again.

"One last thing," he said, "and I promise I'll stop. I won't talk about this again unless you ask. You'll see I live normally. Birds and animals may seem strangely friendly with me, like that moorhen, but otherwise I'm just the same. I'll walk with you, ride, play golf, chat about whatever you want. But I wanted to tell you this from the start, so you'd understand where I'm coming from. And there's one more thing."

He paused. A flicker of fear passed through his eyes.

"There will be a final moment," he said. "A powerful moment when I finally know—when I fully understand and accept that I'm not separate from anything else. That you, me, and all things are one. There's no 'I,' no 'you,' no 'it'—only life. I already believe it's true. But when I truly realize it, it will change everything. On that day, I think I'll see Pan himself. Maybe that moment will mean the end of my physical life—but I don't mind. Maybe it will mean stepping into eternal life, right here, right now, forever. When that happens, my dear Darcy, I'll spread a message of joy so strong, so real, that all those gloomy, joyless beliefs—like Puritanism—will disappear like smoke in the sunlight. But first, I need to reach that understanding."

Darcy studied his face carefully.

"You're scared of that moment," he said.

Frank smiled.

"You're right. I am. But when it comes, I hope I'll be ready."

They sat quietly for a little while. Then Darcy stood up.

"You've completely enchanted me, you strange boy," he said. "It feels like you've told me a fairy tale, and now I'm sitting here thinking, 'Please let it be true.'"

"I promise it is," Frank replied.

"And now I know I won't be able to sleep," Darcy added.

Frank looked at him with gentle curiosity, almost like he didn't quite understand.

"Why does that matter?" he asked.

"It matters a lot. I can't stand it when I don't sleep."

"I could make you sleep if I wanted to," Frank said casually, as if the idea bored him.

"Then go ahead and do it."

"Fine. Go to bed. I'll come up in ten minutes."

After Darcy left, Frank stayed behind for a few minutes. He moved the table back under the veranda and turned off the lamp. Then, with quiet, steady steps, he went upstairs and into Darcy's room. Darcy was already in bed, but wide awake. Frank gave him a soft smile, like someone calming a restless child, and sat on the edge of the bed.

"Look at me," he said, and Darcy did.

Frank spoke softly.

"The birds are asleep in the bushes. The wind is resting. The sea is sleeping too—its waves are just the rising and falling of its breath. The stars move slowly, rocking in the cradle of the sky, and—"

He stopped, leaned over, gently blew out the candle, and left the room. Darcy was already fast asleep.

The next morning, Darcy woke up with a rush of clear, practical thinking, as bright and sharp as the sunlight pouring into the room. As he stretched and got up, he started piecing together the events of the night before. It had all been a trick—some kind of basic hypnotism. That had to be it. The strange ideas, the wild talk, even his own excitement—it had all been caused by the strong will of that strange, glowing young man. The way he'd fallen asleep so quickly after Frank told him to—that proved it. Darcy felt sure he'd been under a spell, and now he was grounded again, filled with good old-fashioned common sense as he went downstairs for breakfast.

Frank was already eating, cheerfully spooning porridge into his mouth with a healthy appetite.

"Sleep well?" he asked.

"Of course," Darcy replied. "Where did you learn to hypnotize people?"

"By the river," Frank said, smiling.

"You really said a lot of crazy stuff last night," Darcy said, sounding firmly logical.

"I know. I got a bit carried away," Frank admitted. "Look—I even remembered to order a terrible newspaper for you. Now you can read about the stock market, or politics, or cricket scores."

Darcy stared at him. In the bright morning light, Frank looked even younger, more full of life, than he had the night before. Something about his presence made Darcy's logical thoughts feel a little less solid.

"You're the strangest person I've ever met," Darcy said. "I still have questions. I want to understand more."

"Ask anything you like," Frank said.

Over the next few days, Darcy kept asking questions—challenging Frank, pointing out flaws, trying to make sense of it all. Slowly, he pulled from Frank a complete version of his beliefs and experiences.

In short, Frank believed that by opening himself completely—what he called "lying naked"—to the same force that moves the stars, forms the waves, causes trees to grow and people to fall in love, he had discovered something most people never even imagine. He felt that, little by little, he was becoming one with that power—the energy behind all living things, the spirit of nature, of force, or what some might call God.

He admitted that others would probably call him a pagan. But for him, it was enough to know that this force existed. He didn't worship it, or pray to it, or praise it. He just knew it was real, in everything—people, trees, animals—and his only goal was to fully understand that it was all the same thing.

Now and then, Darcy would speak up with concern.

"Be careful," he said once. "Wasn't seeing Pan supposed to bring death?"

At that, Frank would simply raise his eyebrows.

"What does it matter?" Frank said. "Sure, the Greeks were right about a lot of things, and they believed this too. But there's something else to consider. The closer I get to it, the more alive, stronger, and younger I become."

"So what do you think will happen when the final moment comes?" Darcy asked.

"I've already told you," Frank said. "It will make me immortal."

Darcy didn't really come to understand Frank's beliefs through their talks. It was more through watching how Frank lived his life.

One morning, they were walking down the village street when an old woman, hunched over but beaming with happiness, shuffled out of her cottage. Frank immediately stopped.

"My dear old friend! How are you?" he called warmly.

She didn't say anything at first. She just stared at his face, as if soaking up the light and joy he gave off. Then she reached out and placed her wrinkled hands on his shoulders.

"You're pure sunshine," she said.

Frank smiled, kissed her forehead gently, and they continued on.

But just a few steps later, something very different happened. A young child came running toward them, tripped, and fell to the ground, crying loudly. Instantly, Frank's expression turned to horror. He plugged his ears with his fingers and took off running, only stopping once he was far away. Darcy made sure the child wasn't badly hurt, then chased after Frank, confused.

"Don't you have any pity?" he asked once he caught up.

Frank shook his head, frustrated.

"Don't you see?" he said. "Pain, anger, anything ugly like that pulls me backwards. It slows me down from reaching what I'm meant for. Maybe when the time comes, I'll understand how it all fits together. But right now, I can't."

"But that old woman," Darcy said. "Wasn't she ugly too?"

Frank's face lit up again.

"No, not at all. She wanted joy. She knew it when she saw it. That's what matters."

Another question crossed Darcy's mind.

"What about Christianity then?" he asked.

"I can't accept it," Frank said. "I can't believe that a religion centered on God—who should be pure joy—could be based on suffering. Maybe it happened in some way I can't understand. But I can't make sense of it, so I leave it alone. My focus is on joy."

They reached the weir above the village, where the loud rush of the river filled the air. Trees dipped their thin branches into the clear water, and the meadow was scattered with summer flowers. Larks flew high into the bright sky, singing, and the world around them seemed alive with music and color.

Frank, as usual, had no hat, his coat slung over one arm and his shirt sleeves rolled up. He stood there like a wild, beautiful creature, his eyes half-closed and mouth slightly open, breathing in the warm, sweet air. Then, without warning, he dropped face-first onto the grass at the river's edge. He buried his face among the daisies and cowslips, stretching out wide with his hands gently pressing into the damp plants.

Darcy had never seen him like this before. Frank's whole body seemed to pulse with a different kind of life, one that went deeper than anything normal. And somehow, a little of that strange, powerful feeling reached Darcy too, and for a brief moment, he truly understood how real Frank's beliefs were.

Suddenly Frank's body tensed. He lifted his head slightly.

"The Pan-pipes," he whispered. "They're so close—so close."

Slowly and carefully, he raised himself onto one elbow. His eyes opened wide, his lids drooping a little as if he were focusing on something far away. A huge, trembling smile spread across his face, full of happiness too deep for words. He stayed like that, perfectly still, for several minutes. Then the look faded, and he lowered his head in peace.

"That was amazing," he said. "How could you not hear it? You poor thing—you really didn't hear anything?"

Spending a week living outdoors with Frank, surrounded by fresh air and sunshine, quickly brought Darcy back to full health. His energy and strength returned, but so did his growing sense that Frank's influence over him was getting stronger. Over and over, he would find himself thinking, "It's impossible. It can't be real." Yet the fact that he had to keep reminding himself showed that part of him was already believing.

After all, the truth was right there in front of him: a boy full of life and energy, standing on the edge of manhood, who somehow, unbelievably, was thirty-five years old. And yet there he was—real, alive, and undeniable.

July began with a few days of strong wind and heavy rain. Darcy didn't want to get sick, so he stayed inside. But Frank didn't seem to care about the weather at all. He kept living just like he did in the sunny days of June—lying in his hammock, walking through the wet grass, or exploring the forest. Birds followed him from tree to tree. He would come home soaked through, but still smiling and full of energy.

"Catch a cold?" Frank said once. "I think I've forgotten how. Sleeping outside all the time makes you tougher. People who stay indoors remind me of peeled fruit—too soft."

"You mean you slept outside last night in all that rain?" Darcy asked. "Where?"

Frank thought for a second.

"I slept in the hammock until almost sunrise," he said. "I remember seeing the sky start to get light. Then I walked to that meadow where we heard the Pan-pipes last week. You remember? Anyway, I always bring a blanket if it's wet."

And he whistled as he went upstairs.

Hearing that, Darcy really started to realize just how strange and wonderful Frank's life had become. Sleeping outside in storms, waking up in the middle of the night, wandering through the woods just for joy—Frank lived a life completely different from anyone else.

That night at dinner, while they were chatting about random things, Darcy suddenly stopped talking.

"I figured it out," he said. "I finally know what's wrong with your idea."

"Well, congratulations," Frank said. "What is it?"

Darcy leaned forward.

"Nature is full of pain and suffering. Every living thing either eats or gets eaten. But in your dream of becoming one with nature, you pretend that suffering doesn't exist. You run from it. And you're waiting for some big final moment."

Frank's face grew serious.

"Well?" he asked.

"Don't you see?" Darcy said. "If you really get that final moment, maybe it won't be happiness. Maybe it'll be horror. Maybe you'll see all the pain and suffering in the world. You've been trying to ignore it."

Frank raised his hand.

"Wait. Let me think."

They sat in silence for a minute.

"That never crossed my mind," Frank said. "Maybe you're right. Maybe the final thing I'll see is all the suffering. Maybe seeing Pan really means seeing all the hidden pain of the world."

He got up and came closer to Darcy.

"If that's true, I'll still go through with it," he said. "Because I'm close now—closer than ever. Today the Pan-pipes played almost all day long. I even heard something moving in the bushes. I saw branches part, and I think I saw a face—not a human face. But I didn't run away."

He walked to the window and looked out into the night.

"Yes, suffering is everywhere," he said. "And I've ignored it. Maybe the final moment will show me all of it. But it's too late to turn back now. Even if I could, I wouldn't. Whatever happens, I know it will be God."

The rain didn't last long. Soon the sun came back, and Darcy and Frank spent long days outside again. It got hotter and hotter, and Frank's energy grew stronger every day.

But, like always in England, the weather changed again. One evening, dark clouds built up in the west. The sun set behind thick thunderclouds, and the air felt heavy and still, like the whole world was holding its breath. Lightning flashed far away, and thunder rolled softly. When bedtime came, the storm hadn't moved closer, but the low rumble of thunder was constant. Darcy, tired and hot, fell into a heavy, restless sleep.

Suddenly, he woke up with a loud crash of thunder shaking the house. He sat up in bed, heart pounding. For a moment, everything was silent except for the rain hissing against the windows. Then, from somewhere outside, a scream tore through the night.

It was a scream full of fear and pain.

It came again. Then he heard a voice he knew, crying out:

"My God! Oh, my God! Oh, Christ!"

Then there was a strange, awful laugh. Then silence again, just the sound of rain.

It all happened in a few seconds. Without thinking, Darcy jumped out of bed, didn't bother with clothes or a light, and rushed to the door. As he opened it, he ran straight into the servant, who was carrying a lamp.

"Did you hear that?" Darcy asked quickly.

The man's face was pale with fear.

"Yes, sir," he said. "That was the master's voice."

They hurried downstairs together, through the dining room where breakfast had already been set, and out onto the terrace. The rain had completely stopped, like someone had shut off the sky. It wasn't totally dark because the moon was still shining somewhere behind the thick clouds.

Darcy ran into the garden with the servant right behind him, carrying a candle. His own huge shadow stretched across the lawn in front of him. The air smelled strong of roses, lilies, wet dirt, and something sharp and bitter that reminded him of an old mountain cabin he once stayed in.

In the dim light and with the flickering candle behind him, Darcy saw the hammock where Frank usually rested. He spotted a flash of white—someone was sitting there—and a dark shape was lying across it. As Darcy got closer, the strange smell grew stronger.

He was only a few steps away when the dark shadow suddenly jumped into the air. Darcy heard hard hoofs tapping on the brick path, and whatever it was bounced away into the bushes. When it was gone, Darcy could see more clearly—someone really was sitting up in the hammock.

For a second, Darcy froze with fear. Then, when the servant caught up to him, they walked to the hammock together.

It was Frank. He wore just a shirt and trousers and sat up stiffly, holding himself with his arms. For a moment, he stared past them, not seeing them. His face was twisted with terrible fear. His upper lip pulled back so far that his gums showed, and his eyes were wide and full of horror. His nostrils flared like he was gasping for air, and deep lines of fear and pain were carved into his face.

Then, right in front of them, Frank's body fell back, and the hammock creaked under him.

Darcy quickly lifted Frank out of the hammock and carried him into the house. For a second, Darcy thought Frank's body moved a little, but when they got inside, he knew there was no life left.

But now Frank's face was peaceful. The terrible look of fear was gone. He looked like a tired boy smiling in his sleep. His eyes were closed, and his mouth curved softly, just like it had when he had smiled that morning in the meadow, hearing the music of the Pan-pipes.

Then they noticed something even stranger.

Frank had come back from swimming before dinner, wearing only his usual shirt and trousers. He hadn't changed. Darcy remembered how, during dinner, Frank rolled up his sleeves because it was hot, and later unbuttoned his shirt a little to cool off.

Now, as they looked at him, the sleeves were still rolled up and the shirt still open—and strange marks were starting to appear on his skin. They grew clearer every second until they could see what they were: deep pointed marks, like hoof prints, as if a huge goat had jumped and stamped on him.

Between the Lights

All day long, snow had fallen without stopping, from sunrise until the faint light outside slowly faded, showing that the sun had set again. But even with the heavy snow, there was no shortage of fun at Everard Chandler's house, where I often spent Christmas—and was spending it again now. The hours passed so quickly it surprised us.

After breakfast, we had a short billiard tournament, while those who weren't playing passed the time with badminton or reading the morning papers. After lunch, most of us spent the afternoon playing a huge game of hide-and-seek all over the house, except for the billiard room, which was off-limits for anyone who wanted some peace. But hardly anyone did—the Christmas spirit had turned us all into kids again. We tiptoed through the dim hallways, jumping at every corner, half expecting someone to leap out at us.

Later, tired but happy, we all gathered for tea in the main hall, a big shadowy room lined with wooden panels. The only light came from a roaring fire made of peat and logs, flickering against the walls. After tea, the tradition of telling ghost stories began. We turned off the electric lights, so everyone could imagine whatever they wanted lurking in the dark corners, and we took turns trying to outdo each other with stories of blood, bones, skeletons, and scary noises.

I had just finished telling my story and was feeling pretty pleased with myself, thinking the worst was over, when Everard spoke. He hadn't told a story yet, and when I looked at him sitting across from me in the firelight, I was surprised. After his illness in the fall, he still looked pale and a little weak, but earlier that day, he had been one of the boldest explorers during our game of hide-and-seek. Now, though, something serious had come over his face.

"I don't really mind that kind of ghost story," he said. "Screams and skeletons are almost boring now. They're familiar. If one of them showed up, I could just hide under the blankets and feel safe."

"But in my story, the skeleton pulled the blankets away!" I said, defending myself.

"I know," he said, smiling a little. "But even that doesn't scare me much. Look around—there are seven or eight skeletons right here, sitting by the fire, dressed in skin and blood like the rest of us. No, real fear—the kind from childhood—was scarier. You didn't even know what you were afraid of. That's what made it so terrifying. If only we could feel that again—"

Mrs. Chandler jumped up from her seat.

"Oh, Everard, you don't really want to feel that again, do you?" she said. "Once was enough!"

This was too good to pass up. Everyone begged him to go on. A real, first-hand ghost story was rare and precious.

Everard laughed. "No, dear, I don't want to feel it again," he said to his wife. Then to the rest of us, "But the thing I'm thinking of—it wasn't much, really. No drama, no ghosts, no skeletons. You'll probably all say it was nothing at all. But it terrified me. I only saw something for a second, and heard something that could have just been a stone falling."

"Still, tell us about the falling stone," I said.

There was a shift in the group around the fire, and it wasn't just people moving their chairs. It felt like the light-hearted fun we had been having all day suddenly faded away. Earlier, we had played hide-and-seek like kids, laughing and running. But now it felt like we were stepping into something real—real fear, real darkness. Mrs. Chandler's worried voice added to the feeling.

"Oh, Everard, are you sure it won't upset you?" she asked as she sat down again.

The room stayed dim, lit only by the occasional burst of flames from the fire. The shadows in the corners seemed deeper now. Everard, who had been sitting in the bright light, was now hidden by the darkness after a burning log collapsed. We could only hear his voice—steady but slow—as he spoke from his low chair.

"Last year," he said, "on December twenty-fourth, Amy and I were here, like always, for Christmas. Some of you were here too—three or four of you."

I was one of them, but I stayed silent. It didn't seem like he needed anyone to answer. He continued without stopping.

"Those of you who were here," he said, "will remember how unusually warm it was that day. We even played croquet on the lawn. It was a little cold for it, honestly, but we played just so we could say we did."

Then he turned and spoke to all of us, sitting still and listening in the flickering firelight.

"We played short games," Everard said, "just like we played billiards today. It was just as warm on the lawn that day as it was in the billiard room this morning. And now, there's probably three feet of snow outside. Maybe even more. Listen."

A sudden gust of wind came down the chimney, and the fire flared up. We heard the snow hitting the windows, soft but steady, like lots of tiny feet running past. It sounded like hundreds of little people gathering outside. Some of us turned and looked at the windows. They were small and had thick bars across them. Snow had piled up on the bars, but there was nothing else to see.

"Yes, last Christmas Eve was warm and sunny," Everard went on. "There hadn't even been a frost yet, and one last dahlia flower was still blooming. I always thought that flower must have been a little crazy."

He paused.

"And maybe I was a little crazy too," he added.

Nobody said anything. His story had caught everyone's full attention. It fit the strange feeling of the snowy night perfectly. Mrs. Chandler shifted in her seat, but no one else moved. In just a few minutes, we had gone from laughing and playing like kids to sitting silent and serious.

"I was sitting out," Everard said to me, "while you and my wife were playing your croquet match. Then suddenly, I felt cold and shivered. I looked up—and I didn't see you two anymore. I saw something else. Something I really hope had nothing to do with you."

At that moment, Everard had all of us hooked. We couldn't look away.

"You know the croquet lawn," he said. "It's surrounded by flowers and a brick wall. There's only one gate. Well, when I looked up, it felt like the lawn was shrinking, and the walls were closing in. They also got taller. The sky started to darken until it was almost completely black, except for a little bit of light coming through the gate.

"There was that dahlia flower still standing, and I stared at it, desperate for something familiar. But it changed. The red flower became a dim red fire.

"Then everything changed completely. I wasn't outside anymore—I was inside a small, low-roofed round room, like an old animal shed. The ceiling beams were just above my head. It was dark, except for a little bit of light coming from a door across from me. I could tell it led outside, but hardly any fresh air came in. The air inside smelled terrible, like a place full of people that hadn't been cleaned for years. But the worst part wasn't the smell—it was the awful feeling, like something truly evil was there. The people—or whatever they were—seemed more like animals than humans. I also felt like I had been thrown far back in time."

He paused again, and the firelight lit up everyone's faces. We were all staring at him, waiting for what would come next.

"Where the dahlia had been, there was now a low fire," he said. "Shapes were sitting around it. At first, I couldn't see clearly. Then either my eyes adjusted, or the fire got brighter, and I saw that they were small people. One of them stood up, and even standing, he barely cleared the low roof. He wore a shirt that went down to his knees, but his arms were bare and hairy. They started pointing at me and chattering.

"That's when I realized I couldn't move. I was completely paralyzed. I couldn't lift my arms or turn my head. I even tried to scream, but no sound came out. I was trapped there, helpless.

"Then, just like that, it was over. I was back on the croquet lawn. You and my wife hadn't even played your shot yet. But I was sweating and shaking all over.

"You might say I just fell asleep and had a nightmare. Maybe. But I didn't feel tired before, and I didn't feel sleepy after. It was like someone had opened a book to show me a page of horror, and then snapped it shut."

Suddenly someone jumped up and switched on the electric light. It made me flinch, but honestly, I was glad.

Everard laughed.

"I feel like Hamlet in the play," he said. "As if someone here knows exactly what I'm talking about. Should I keep going?"

Nobody answered. But Everard kept telling his story anyway.

"Well, let's just say it wasn't really a dream, but more like a hallucination," Everard said. "Either way, it stayed with me. For months, it was always in the back of my mind. Sometimes it was quiet, but other times it would stir and remind me it was still there. It didn't help to tell myself it was nothing. It felt like something dark had planted itself deep inside me and was slowly growing.

"It didn't exactly make me sick. I still ate and slept normally. But every morning, I would wake up all of a sudden, not slowly like usual, and feel this deep, terrible sadness. Even when I was eating or drinking, sometimes I would stop and wonder if it was worth it.

"Eventually, I told two people what was bothering me. I hoped that talking about it might help, or that maybe someone could tell me it was just something simple like bad digestion. I told my wife, who just laughed at me. Then I told my doctor, who also laughed and said I was healthier than most people. He said a change of place might help and promised me I wasn't going crazy.

"After that, we went to London for the season, just like always. Nothing happened there to remind me of that Christmas Eve. But the memory didn't fade—it only grew stronger. Instead of feeling like a dream, it became even sharper, almost like it was burning itself into my mind.

"After London, we went to Scotland.

"That year, for the first time, I rented a small forest in Sutherland called Glen Callan. It was very wild and far away from everything, but it had great deer hunting. It wasn't far from the sea, and the guides always warned me to carry a compass because sea-mists could come in quickly and trap you for hours. At first, I always took my compass. But after a few weeks of perfect weather, I got lazy and often left it at home.

"One day, we went hunting in a part of the forest I didn't know well. It was a high, flat area, with a steep drop to a lake on one side and a gentler slope down to a river on the other. My guide insisted we climb the steep cliffs from the lake side, because of the way the wind was blowing. I didn't agree—it seemed like we could have taken an easier path without scaring the deer—but he insisted, so I gave in.

"The climb was terrible. We had to scramble over huge rocks, with deep holes hidden under patches of heather. Every step needed to be careful. There were snakes too—we saw at least a dozen adders on the way up—and I really hate snakes. But after two hours of hard climbing, we reached the top.

"Unfortunately, the guide had been wrong. The deer must have smelled us and were already gone. He blamed it on the wind changing, but I didn't believe him. I thought maybe he had another reason for taking the harder path, though I didn't know what it could be.

"Still, we were lucky. About an hour later, we spotted another group of deer, and around two o'clock, I managed to shoot a big stag. After that, I sat down on the heather, ate my lunch, and enjoyed a rest in the sun. The pony, carrying the stag, had already started back toward the lodge."

"The morning had been strangely warm, with a little breeze blowing off the sea, which sparkled a few miles away under a blue haze. Even with the awful climb we had that morning, I had felt unusually peaceful. A few times, I even checked myself inside, wondering if that old fear was still there. But it barely stirred. Since Christmas, I hadn't felt so free of it. Lying there on the grass, looking up at the blue sky and watching the smoke from my cigarette curl away, I felt completely calm.

"But I didn't get to rest for long. Sandy came up and asked me to move. He said the weather had changed—the wind had shifted—and he wanted me off the high ground because a sea mist was coming in fast.

"'And that's a bad place to be if the mist hits,' he said, pointing at the cliffs we had climbed earlier.

"I stared at him, confused. There was an easy way down toward the river on our right. We didn't have to go near those cliffs again. I was sure he had some other reason for wanting to avoid the safer path. Still, one thing was clear: the mist really was coming in, and when I checked my pockets, I realized I had left my compass behind.

"Then we wasted precious time arguing. I insisted on taking the easy way. Sandy begged me to trust him and go back over the rocks. He gave the most ridiculous excuses: that the easier way was too mossy (even though it had been dry for weeks), or that it was too long, or that there were too many snakes. None of it made sense. Finally, tired of arguing, I started walking toward the gentle slope and told him to follow me without another word. He came after me, but he wasn't happy about it.

"We weren't even halfway down when the mist hit us. It rushed up from the valley like a breaking wave, and in just a few minutes we were wrapped in thick fog. We could barely see a dozen yards ahead. Still, I felt glad we weren't stuck climbing those cliffs again. I also felt proud of myself for leading the way, confident we would soon find the river path.

"More than anything, I was happy because, for the first time in months, I felt no fear. I felt as free as a schoolboy starting summer vacation.

"But the mist got thicker, and soon it started raining—or maybe the fog was just that wet. I got soaked to the bone. I had never been so wet in my life. And still, we didn't find the river path. Sandy muttered behind me, staying close, like he was afraid.

"There are bad companions in this world, and a frightened man is one of the worst. Fear spreads easily, and soon I started feeling nervous too. On top of that, the ground felt strange. Sometimes it seemed flat, other times like we were climbing again, even though we should have been going downhill. It started to get dark too—it was October after all—but I remembered that the full moon would rise soon.

"Then it got colder, and the rain turned into steady snowfall.

"Things were looking bad. But then I heard the river off to the left. It should have been straight ahead, so we were off track, but at least it gave us something to aim for. I turned left and headed toward it.

"But after walking only a little way, I heard a strange cry behind me and turned just in time to see Sandy running away into the mist. I called after him, but he didn't answer. I could only hear the sound of stones kicked up by his running.

"I didn't know what had scared him, but with him gone, I actually felt better—his fear wasn't dragging me down anymore. I kept walking toward the river, feeling almost cheerful.

"Then, suddenly, I saw a dark shape in front of me. Before I could even think, I found myself climbing up a steep grassy slope.

"The wind had picked up, and the snow was blowing hard now. But the dark shape seemed like shelter, and I was drawn to it. I climbed higher, and soon I saw a wall about twelve feet tall. Right where I reached it, there was a hole or a doorway with a faint light inside.

"I bent down and went through the low tunnel. After a few yards, I came out the other side just as the sky got a little brighter—the mist was thinning and the moon was trying to shine through.

"I found myself inside a round stone enclosure. About four feet up the walls were broken stones, like the remains of an old floor.

"And then two things happened at once.

"First, all the fear that had haunted me since Christmas came rushing back. I knew this was the place I had seen in my vision. Second, I saw a small figure—only about three and a half feet tall—creeping toward me.

"I could hear it stumble on a rock. The air around me smelled horribly rotten. My whole soul filled with sick dread. I tried to scream but couldn't. I tried to run but was frozen.

"But somehow, the terror gave me strength. I finally broke free, screamed, and bolted through the passageway. I ran down the slope and didn't stop. I didn't care where I was going—I just needed to get away.

"Luckily, I soon found the river path and after another hour, I reached the lodge.

"The next day, I caught a terrible chill and ended up with pneumonia. I was stuck in bed for six weeks.

"That's the story," Everard finished. "There are plenty of ways to explain it. Maybe I fell asleep on the lawn at Christmas and my mind brought it back when I found myself lost in an old ruined fort, with a sheep or goat moving around inside. There are hundreds of simple explanations.

"But still—it was a strange coincidence. And anyone who believes in second sight might find it interesting."

"And that's it?" I asked.

"Yes," he said. "And honestly, it was almost too much for me. I think the dressing bell just rang."

Outside the Door

The rest of the group staying with my friend Geoffrey Aldwych at his old house near a small village north of Sheringham had gone off after dinner to play cards and billiards. For now, Mrs. Aldwych and I were left alone in the drawing-room. We were sitting across from each other at a small round table, trying—without success—to get it to move. Even though we had tried patiently for a long time, the table hadn't budged at all. It sat there as still as a rock. Not even a small shake.

After a while, we gave up and started talking about psychic stuff instead. I joked that if we couldn't even move a tiny table, we had no chance of moving anything. But just as I said that, there was a sudden, loud knock from the table. It made us both jump.

"What was that?" I asked.

"Just a knock," she said. "I thought something might happen."

"Do you really believe it was a spirit?" I asked.

"Oh, no," she said. "I don't think it had anything to do with spirits."

"Maybe it was just because of the dry weather," I said.

But honestly, it didn't sound like wood creaking. It was a loud, sharp sound, not a dry crack.

"No, I don't think it was the weather either," she said, smiling. "I think it happened because we were trying so hard to move the table. Does that sound silly?"

"A little," I said. "But you're good at making things sound reasonable."

"That's not very nice," she said, laughing.

"It's meant as a compliment. Please explain more."

"Let's go outside," she said. "It's a warm night, and—"

"And the dark is perfect for spooky things," I joked.

"My ideas aren't spooky," she said. "They're more about real, physical things."

We walked out into the cool night air. The last bits of sunset had faded. The moon hadn't risen yet, and the sea was quiet. A soft breeze brought the smell of salt and flowers. White moths floated over the dark garden. We walked past the house and into the shadows of shaped hedges, finding chairs near a striped tent by the old bowling green.

"Okay," I said. "Tell me your theory—and a story too if you have one."

"You want a real ghost story too?" she asked.

"Yes, if possible."

"Well, you're in luck," she said. "I'll tell you my idea first, and then a true story that happened right here."

"I'm ready," I said.

She waited while I lit a cigarette. Then she started speaking clearly and calmly. Sitting there in the dark, her voice sounded extra sharp and easy to follow.

"We're only starting to realize," she said, "how deeply the mind is connected to the physical world. Doctors have known for a long time that emotions affect the body. Fear can speed up your heart. Anger changes your blood. Worry upsets your stomach. Even strong emotions can make you do things you normally couldn't.

"That's just the mind affecting the body. But maybe the mind can affect other things too—like wood or stone."

"Like table-turning?" I asked.

"Exactly," she said. "Sometimes we can send out invisible forces without even knowing how. We tried to move the table just now, and even though it didn't move, that loud knock happened afterward. I think it was caused by our efforts."

She paused, and I nodded.

"To me, it feels natural that the mind can touch the world outside of us. We don't really understand how it works, just like we don't know exactly how a message travels through the air without wires. But it happens. Maybe our inner energy can move into other things—whether that's our own bodies or even objects we think of as dead, like tables."

She paused again before continuing.

"Sometimes," she continued, "the energy that passes from us into objects can show itself in strange ways. When we focus on a table, for example, that energy might make it move or create sounds. The table soaks up some of our force, almost like a battery being charged. I've seen it happen many times—a table or chair moving on its own, but only when it had been filled with that energy.

"This reminds me a lot of haunted houses. In places where a terrible crime or powerful emotion happened, there seems to be a leftover imprint. In these houses, people sometimes hear noises or see things like footsteps or ghostly figures. It's like the house itself holds onto the memory, and under the right conditions, it plays it back—just like a record player repeats sounds that were once spoken into it."

"That's all just theory," I said.

"Maybe," she replied. "But it explains a lot of strange things. Otherwise, we have to believe something worse—that the spirit of a murdered person is forced to relive their death over and over again, making their suffering visible to us. I can't believe that. But my idea—that the house itself holds onto the memory—is easier to accept. Does that make sense?"

"It makes sense," I said. "But now I want proof. Tell me the story you promised."

"I will," she said. Then she began her story.

"It was about a year ago when Jack bought this house from Mrs. Denison. Both of us had heard rumors that the house was haunted, but we didn't know any details. Last month, I had my own experience. Then, when Mrs. Denison visited us last week, I asked her about it—and what she said matched what happened to me. I'll tell you first what happened to me, then what she said.

"One month ago, Jack went away for a few days, and I stayed here alone. One Sunday night, feeling perfectly healthy and cheerful, I went up to bed around eleven. My room is on the first floor, right at the bottom of the stairs that lead up to the second floor. There are four other rooms along my hallway, but they were all empty that night. Across the landing at the far end were more bedrooms, but they too were empty. I was the only person sleeping on that floor.

"My bed is right behind my door, and there's a light above it, controlled by a switch next to the bed. Another switch there turns on the hallway light outside. Jack set it up that way so you could light the hall before stepping out into the dark.

"I usually sleep very soundly. It's rare for me to wake up during the night. But that night I woke up suddenly, and worse, I was terrified. I didn't know why. I tried to reason with myself, but it didn't help. Fear was wrapped all around me, cold and tight.

"So I turned on the light and tried to calm myself by reading the book I had brought to bed. It was 'The Green Carnation'—not exactly a scary book. But even reading didn't help. I felt just as scared, maybe even more. After a few pages, I gave up, turned off the light, and tried to sleep. I checked the time first—it was ten minutes to two.

"But lying there in the dark made things worse. My fear grew clearer, like something bad was getting closer. I could feel it coming, even though I couldn't see or hear anything yet. Then the clock struck two. I heard its chiming, and a second later, the stable clock outside struck the hour more loudly.

"I lay frozen, heart pounding. Then I heard footsteps just outside my door, coming from the stairs that led up to the second floor. It was the sound of someone moving carefully in the dark—footsteps shuffling and a hand feeling along the banister. The footsteps reached my door. I heard the brush of clothes against the wood, and fingers fumbling over the door handle. My fear almost made me scream.

"Then I thought—maybe it's just a servant who's sick or looking for something. But the slow, dragging footsteps and the groping hand didn't feel right. Still, trying to be brave, I turned on both the light in my room and the hallway light. I opened the door and looked out.

"The hallway was brightly lit from one end to the other, but it was completely empty. And yet, as I stood there, I could still hear the shuffling footsteps moving away down the hall, even though there was no one there. The sound faded into the distance, turning into the side gallery at the end of the passage.

"And just like that, all my fear vanished. It had been the invisible walker I was afraid of. Once it was gone, so was my terror. I went back to bed and slept peacefully until morning."

Mrs. Aldwych paused again, and I stayed quiet. Somehow, the horror of her story came from how simple it was. She continued almost right away.

"Now for what happened next," she said, "or at least what I believe explains it. Mrs. Denison, the former owner of the house, visited us not long ago. I mentioned that we had heard the house was supposed to be haunted, and I asked her to tell me the story. Here's what she said:

'Back in 1610, the heiress to the property, Helen Denison, was engaged to marry a young man named Lord Southern. If she had children, the property would leave the Denison family. But if she died without children, the estate would pass to her cousin. A week before the wedding, her cousin and his brother rode here after dark, found their way to her room on the second floor, gagged her, and tried to kill her. She managed to escape, feeling her way along the passage and into the room at the end of the gallery. But they caught up to her there and killed her. The truth came out later when the younger brother confessed.'"

Mrs. Aldwych went on, "Mrs. Denison said that no one had ever actually seen a ghost here, but people sometimes heard footsteps on the stairs or along the passage. And it only ever happened between two and three in the morning—the same time when the murder had taken place."

"Have you heard it again since that first night?" I asked.

"Yes, a few times," she said. "But it's never frightened me again. I was only scared because I didn't know what it was."

"I think I'd be more afraid if I did know," I said.

"I don't think you would be," she answered. "Once you understand it, there's nothing really shocking about it. You know my theory already—"

"Please explain how your theory fits this," I said.

"It's simple," she said. "That poor girl, terrified and desperate, stumbled down the hallway, probably hearing her killers coming closer. The intense fear and emotion she felt somehow left an imprint on the house. Sensitive people—those who are tuned in, like radios picking up invisible signals—can sometimes pick it up. But the marks are always there, just like waves from a radio broadcast are always in the air, even when no one is listening. If you believe in brainwaves at all, the idea isn't that strange."

"So the brainwave stays there forever?" I asked.

"Every wave leaves a mark," she said. "If you don't believe it, I could offer you a room right along the path where the poor girl ran."

I stood up.

"No, thanks," I said. "I'm perfectly happy where I am."

The Terror by Night

The way people pass emotions to each other is so common that most of us don't even notice it anymore. It feels as normal as opening a window to let fresh air into a stuffy room. No one is surprised when a cheerful person walks into a sad room and suddenly everyone feels a little better. We don't really know how this happens. But with things like wireless communication now part of everyday life—like getting news while crossing the ocean—it doesn't seem crazy to think emotions could travel in a similar invisible way.

Even when we read something emotional in a book, it can make us laugh or cry, even though it's just words on a page. So maybe the mind can reach out to other minds just as easily.

Sometimes, though, stranger things happen—things people might call ghosts, tricks, or nonsense. Maybe it's easier just to call them "emotions that got left behind." Some ghosts are seen, some are heard, and some are even felt. There are even stories about feeling cold, heat, or strange smells.

Maybe all of us are like radio receivers that sometimes catch emotional "signals" floating around us. Most of the time we don't tune in clearly, but once in a while, we pick up a strong message. The story I'm about to tell is interesting because several people seemed to receive the same emotional "signal" at the same time. This happened ten years ago, but I wrote it all down when it was fresh.

Jack Lorimer had been a close friend of mine for years before he married my cousin. Even after the wedding, we stayed just as close. Not long after they married, Jack's wife, Daisy, found out she had tuberculosis. She was sent to Davos, a mountain town known for helping people recover, and her sister went with her. The doctors caught it early, and everyone was hopeful she would get better.

That November, Jack and I spent Christmas with them in Davos. Week after week, Daisy's health kept improving. Jack and I needed to be back in London by the end of January, but Daisy stayed longer to finish recovering.

On the day we left, she and her sister came to the station. I'll never forget Daisy's last words:

"Oh, don't look so sad, Jack. You'll see me again soon."

Then the little mountain train whistled, and we left.

London in February was miserable—foggy, wet, and bitterly cold. It felt much worse than the clear, sunny cold of the mountains. Jack and I both felt lonely, so we decided it was silly to keep two separate houses open. We lived on the same street anyway. We flipped a coin to decide whose house to stay in. My house won.

About ten days after we got back, even though we kept getting great letters from Davos, a strange feeling of fear hit Jack—and then me too. Maybe I caught it from him, or maybe we both felt it separately. But it was true that it didn't hit me until after he talked about it.

One night, when we were saying goodnight, Jack said,

"I've felt awful all day," he said. "And after getting such good news from Daisy, too. I don't know why."

He poured himself a drink.

"Probably just your liver," I joked. "You shouldn't drink that—give it to me instead."

"No, I feel perfectly fine," he said.

As he talked, I opened a letter and got excited.

"Hey, great news!" I said. "Someone wants to rent your house for five guineas a week until Easter!"

But Jack didn't look excited at all.

"Thanks. But I don't think I can stay here until Easter," he said.

"Why not? Daisy even told me to convince you to stay. She says it'll be more cheerful for you."

Jack agreed slowly.

"Okay, I'll stay," he said. Then he walked up and down the room, clearly unsettled.

"It's not me," he said. "It's something. Some awful feeling—like the 'terror by night' they talk about in the Bible."

"You're told not to be afraid of that," I said, trying to lighten the mood.

"Easy for the Bible to say," he muttered. "I'm scared. Something bad is coming."

"Five guineas a week are coming," I joked. "And Daisy's getting better every day. Take that to bed with you."

That night, I went to sleep feeling cheerful. But I woke up sometime in the middle of the night, and the "terror by night" Jack had spoken of had found me too.

Fear grabbed hold of me—an awful, paralyzing fear. I didn't know what it was exactly, but it felt like some disaster was heading straight for us, just like you know a storm is coming when you see the pressure drop on a barometer.

Jack noticed it right away when we met at breakfast the next morning. The sky outside was a gloomy brown, not dark enough for lights, but miserable all the same.

"So, it's gotten to you too," he said.

And I couldn't even pretend I was just feeling a little sick. Besides, I had never felt healthier in my life.

For the rest of that day, and the next, the fear stayed with me like a heavy black cloud. I didn't know exactly what I was afraid of, but it was sharp and very close, getting nearer every minute, like a storm spreading across the sky. By the third day, after feeling so helpless, I managed to pull myself together. I thought, either this fear was all in our heads, some trick of nerves—or maybe, somehow, we were picking up a real wave of emotion from somewhere else. Either way, I knew I had to stop giving in to it.

For two days I hadn't done anything except sit and shiver. So I made a plan to keep busy all day and find something fun for the evening.

"We'll have an early dinner," I said, "and then go see The Man from Blankley's. I've already asked Philip to come, and I've gotten tickets. Dinner at seven."

(Philip, by the way, was a longtime friend and a respected doctor.)

Jack put down his newspaper.

"Yeah, you're probably right," he said. "Sitting around doing nothing doesn't help. Did you sleep well?"

"Yes, just fine," I answered, but a little sharply, because I was actually exhausted from hardly sleeping at all.

"Wish I had," he said.

That wouldn't do. I couldn't let us both keep sinking.

"We've got to pull ourselves together," I said. "Look at us—two healthy grown men, acting like scared kids. Maybe the fear is real, maybe it's imaginary, but being afraid is the worst part. There's nothing to fear but fear itself. Let's read our newspapers like normal people. So who do you bet on—Mr. Druce, the Duke of Portland, or the Times Book Club?"

I kept myself busy all day, throwing myself into work. I stayed so late at the office that I had to take a cab home instead of walking. I wanted to be home in time to get dressed for dinner.

But by then, the message—the thing we had been feeling for days—was finally about to break through.

When I got home, Jack was already dressed and waiting in the drawing room. It was almost seven o'clock. Even though the day had been warm and muggy, when I stepped into the house, it suddenly felt bitterly cold—like the crisp, stinging cold we had felt in Switzerland.

There was a fire laid in the fireplace, but it wasn't lit. I went over to light it.

"It's freezing in here," I said. "Servants have no sense. You'd think they'd know to light a fire when it's cold."

"Oh, don't light it!" Jack said quickly. "It's the warmest, muggiest evening I can remember."

I stared at him. My hands were shaking from the cold. Jack noticed.

"You're shivering!" he said. "Are you sick? But the room's not cold—look at the thermometer."

He pointed to the thermometer on the writing desk.

"Sixty-five degrees," he said.

I didn't argue. But at that moment, both of us felt it—something was "coming through." I could feel it deep inside me, like a vibration.

"Hot or cold, I need to get dressed," I said.

Still shaking, I went upstairs. My clothes were already laid out, but there was no hot water, so I rang for my valet. He came quickly, but he looked scared—or at least, he seemed that way to my already-nervous mind.

"What's wrong?" I asked.

"Nothing, sir," he stammered. "You rang?"

"Yes, for hot water. But what's the matter?"

He shuffled nervously.

"I thought... I thought I saw a lady on the stairs," he said. "Coming up right behind me. And I didn't hear the front doorbell."

"Where exactly did you see her?" I asked.

"On the stairs, sir. Then standing outside the drawing-room door, like she didn't know whether to go in."

"Probably just one of the maids," I said. But deep down, I knew it wasn't.

"No, sir. It wasn't one of the servants," he said.

"Then who?"

"I couldn't see clearly, sir. It was dim. But... I thought it looked like Mrs. Lorimer."

"Just get the hot water," I said.

But he hesitated, clearly frightened.

At that moment, the front doorbell rang. It was seven o'clock—Philip had arrived, right on time.

"That's Dr. Enderly," I said. "Maybe you'll be braver with someone else on the stairs."

Then, suddenly, a scream ripped through the house. It was so awful, so full of pure terror, that I froze where I stood. For a moment, I couldn't move. Then, with a huge effort, I forced myself to run downstairs, with my valet close behind me. Philip was already rushing up from the ground floor.

"What was that? What happened?" he shouted.

We ran together into the drawing room.

Jack was lying on the floor in front of the fireplace, his chair overturned beside him. Philip bent down, pulling open Jack's shirt.

"Open all the windows," he said quickly. "The room's full of something."

We threw open every window. To me, hot air rushed in from outside. Philip leaned over Jack for a while, then stood up.

"He's dead," he said. "Leave the windows open. The room's still thick with chloroform."

Slowly, I noticed the room warming up again. To Philip, the drug smell faded. But neither I nor the valet had smelled anything at all.

Two hours later, a telegram arrived from Davos. It asked me to tell Jack that Daisy had died—and it had been sent before Jack died. Daisy's sister said she expected Jack to travel there right away. But he was already gone—two hours before.

The next day, I left for Davos and found out what had happened. Daisy had developed a small abscess that needed a simple operation.

She was nervous about it, so they gave her chloroform. The surgery went fine. She woke up feeling well. But an hour later, she suddenly collapsed and died around 8 PM Davos time—7 PM in London, the same moment Jack died.

She had insisted Jack not be told about the operation, to keep him from worrying.

And that's the end of the story. My servant saw a woman, standing outside the drawing-room door where Jack was, just as Daisy's spirit must have been passing. I felt the cold, the crisp air of Davos. Philip smelled chloroform. And Jack—he must have seen Daisy herself. And he went with her.

The Other Bed

I went to Switzerland just before Christmas, expecting the usual amazing weather — cold but sunny days perfect for skating, and clear nights with fresh, freezing air. Normally, even if it snowed, it only lasted a day or two before the weather turned perfect again.

But this time, the weather was terrible. Every day, strong winds roared through the valley, bringing sleet that turned to snow at night. It didn't stop for ten days. Every night, I checked my barometer, hoping for good news, but the needle just kept dropping until it stayed stuck on "Storm." I mention this because maybe the bad weather was to blame for what happened next. You can decide for yourself.

I had booked a room at the Hôtel Beau Site and was happy to find out that for just twelve francs a day, I got a nice room with two beds. The hotel was packed, so I quickly confirmed the price at the front desk — I didn't want them to realize they made a mistake! The clerk smiled and said I had the right room.

I arrived around three in the afternoon. It was a beautiful, sunny day — the last nice one. I hurried to the rink to skate for a few hours, then went back to the hotel around sunset. I had some letters to write, so I ordered tea and went up to my room, No. 23.

The door was slightly open. As I got close, I thought I heard a faint noise inside. I figured it was my servant unpacking. But when I stepped inside, the room was empty. Everything was neat and ready. I glanced at my barometer and saw, to my disappointment, that the pressure had dropped even more. I quickly forgot about the noise I thought I heard.

The room itself was great: two beds, a big washing stand, a sofa, two armchairs, a writing desk, and even a second table for meals. My window faced east, and I could still see the sunset glowing on the snowy mountains. Above, a thin sliver of moon was rising among the early stars. I drank my tea feeling very pleased with everything.

Then, suddenly, I felt like the beds were wrong. I couldn't sleep in the bed my servant had picked for me. Without thinking, I jumped up and swapped my things to the other bed. Once I did, I felt much better, even though I had no idea why I needed to do it.

I spent about an hour writing letters, feeling more and more sleepy. Since there was still time before dinner, I lay down on the sofa with a book, planning to nap. I fell asleep almost immediately.

While sleeping, I had a strange dream. I dreamed that my servant came quietly into the room. He didn't wake me, but moved around softly, tidying things. The light was very dim, and I couldn't see him clearly, but I just knew it was him. Then he stopped at the washing stand and took out a razor. I saw him sharpening it and testing it on his thumb — then, to my horror, I saw him try it on his own throat.

Suddenly there was a loud crashing noise — the kind that happens in dreams — and I woke up. The door was half open, and my real servant was just stepping inside. The crash must have been the sound of the door opening.

That night, I joined five old friends for dinner. We talked and played bridge, chatting about the weather, skating, and even arguing about card games. Later, while having drinks and smoking one last cigarette, we started talking about ghost stories and strange feelings people sometimes have.

Harry Lambert explained it simply:

"Everything we do — every step we take, every strong feeling we have — leaves a mark on the world," he said. "When something terrible happens, like someone killing themselves or someone else, the emotions can stay in a place for a long time. Sensitive people might feel them. It's like a haunted house."

He laughed and added, "I bet the waiter who served us tonight is a sensitive. He probably feels things like that."

It was getting late, so I stood up and joked,

"Let's hurry him off to a haunted house. As for me, I'm heading to bed!"

Outside, the storm the barometer had warned about had started. A cold, harsh wind rushed through the pine trees and howled around the mountains. Snow had begun to fall, and the sky was dark and heavy. It felt like something unseen was moving around in the night. Still, I tried not to think negatively. If I had to stay indoors for a while, at least I was lucky to have such a nice, comfortable room. I had plenty to do inside, even though I would've much rather been outdoors. And for now, nothing felt better than resting in a real bed after being cramped in a train seat all night.

I was halfway through getting ready for bed when someone knocked. The waiter from dinner came in, holding a bottle of whisky. He was tall, and even though I hadn't noticed him earlier, I immediately understood what my friend Harry meant when he said the man looked like a "sensitive." There was something deep and strange in his eyes—like he could see beyond what was right in front of him.

"The bottle of whisky for you, sir," he said, putting it down.

"I didn't order any whisky," I replied.

He looked confused. "Room twenty-three?" he asked. Then he glanced at the second bed. "Ah, for the other gentleman, of course."

"But I'm alone," I said. "There is no other gentleman."

He picked the bottle back up. "Sorry, sir. I'm new here, just arrived today. I thought…"

"Yes?" I said.

"I thought room twenty-three had ordered a bottle," he repeated. "Good night, sir. My apologies."

I got into bed, turned off the lights, and expected to fall asleep quickly—I was tired and heavy from the stormy weather. But my mind wouldn't settle. It kept circling through little things from the day, like how I thought I heard movement in the room before I entered, or the strange dream I had of someone sharpening a razor, or the waiter's confusion about another guest. I didn't think they were connected; I was just stuck on them like a tired person tripping over the same thought again and again. Then I remembered how strongly I felt that I couldn't sleep in the other bed. Still, no answer came to mind, and I drifted off to sleep.

The next day began a long stretch of terrible weather—snow, sleet, and freezing wind made it impossible to enjoy anything outside. The snow was too soft for sledding, it clumped up on skis, and the skating rink had turned into a slushy mess. That alone was enough to make anyone feel down, but I felt something darker. A heavy sadness and fear hung over me. At first, I didn't know what I was afraid of, but slowly it became clear: I was afraid of my room, especially the second bed. I couldn't explain it, and it seemed silly, but the feeling only grew stronger. It seemed like little, unimportant things added up until my fear had taken a clear shape.

I didn't tell anyone. It sounded ridiculous—just nerves from being stuck inside for too long, I told myself.

But things kept happening. One night, I woke up from a horrible nightmare, panicking because I thought I had somehow ended up in the other bed. A few times, when I got up early to look out the window, I noticed the sheets on that bed looked like they'd been slept in—messed up, then smoothed over just enough to hide it. To calm myself, I set a little "trap" by making the bed neatly and putting the pillow on top. But the next morning, the bed was even more disheveled, and there was a deep dent in the pillow, like someone had laid their head there.

Oddly, these things didn't bother me much during the day. It was only at night, as I got ready for bed, that I felt scared about what else might happen.

Sometimes, when I needed something or rang for help, it was the "Sensitive" who came. But he never came all the way into the room. He would just crack the door open to take my request, and when he came back, he'd leave my boots or whatever else outside the door. Once, I insisted he come in, and as he stepped into the room, I saw him cross himself. He looked terrified. That didn't help my nerves.

Twice he showed up in the evening without being called, just like that first night, to say my bottle of whisky was outside. But I hadn't ordered any. He seemed completely confused, apologizing over and over. "I thought it was for number twenty-three," he said. "Sorry, it's my mistake. It must have been the other guest." Then he paused and corrected himself. "But there is no other guest. That bed is empty."

That night, the strange thing happened again, and this time I couldn't shake the feeling that maybe—just maybe—the other bed wasn't really empty. The awful weather had finally cleared up. Now the moon was full and bright, shining high above the mountains. Everyone at dinner was cheerful, lifted by the sunshine and clear skies. But for me, the fear that had haunted me only grew worse. It felt like a terrible statue had been taking shape in my mind, and soon the final piece would be revealed.

Twice that night I almost went down to the front desk to ask if they could make up a bed for me somewhere else—anywhere—even if it was in the billiard room. But I couldn't bring myself to do it. What was I so afraid of? A dream? Messy bed sheets? A waiter who kept mixing up orders? It felt silly and weak to run away.

Still, I couldn't focus on games or conversation. I needed something to keep my mind busy, so after dinner I went back to my room and started working on proofreading pages. It was boring, but it required full attention. Before I sat down, I checked the room again. Everything looked normal. The wallpaper was covered in cheerful daisies, the wooden floor was polished, the radiator was warm, and both beds were turned down for the night. But when I looked at the other bed, I noticed a strange shadow on the sheet and pillow. It looked almost like a stain.

I felt a sudden rush of fear, but I forced myself to go closer. I touched the spot—it was damp. Then I remembered: I had tossed some wet clothes on the bed before dinner. That must be it. I calmed down and started reading again. My fear faded.

From downstairs I could hear the faint sound of music. People were dancing. Slowly, the music faded. Voices and footsteps echoed in the halls, then doors closed one by one. Soon, the hotel was quiet.

Sometime past midnight, I paused to check the time. I only had a bit more work to do but had run out of paper. I had bought more earlier and left it downstairs. It would only take a minute to fetch it.

As I left the room, the electric light was brighter than before, probably because most of the hotel was dark now. I glanced at the bed again. The stain was still there. I had forgotten about it, but now it made me uneasy. I touched it again. Still damp—but it felt warm and slightly sticky. It didn't feel like water. And right then, I felt it—I wasn't alone in the room.

Now, I'm not a particularly brave person. But this time, curiosity was stronger than fear. I wiped my hand quickly and walked downstairs to the lobby. The "sensitive" night porter was there, half-asleep. He didn't hear me come in, and I quietly picked up my packet of paper. Somehow, seeing him asleep in that chair comforted me. Whatever haunted the other bed, it wasn't calling to him tonight.

Back in my room, I opened the paper package. It was wrapped in an old American newspaper. The date caught my eye—almost a year old. Then I read part of the article:

"The body of Mr. Silas R. Hume, who committed suicide last week at the Hôtel Beau Site, Moulin sur Chalons, is to be returned to Boston, Mass. He died by cutting his throat with a razor during a fit of delirium tremens caused by drinking. Three dozen empty whisky bottles were found in his closet..."

Just then, the lights went out.

The room was pitch black. And I knew—without a doubt—that I was not alone.

My scalp tingled. I could feel something there. Slowly, my eyes adjusted. The shapes of the furniture came into view, dimly lit by the moonlight outside. And then—I saw it.

A figure stood by the sink between the two windows. It moved its hands around the shelf above the basin. Then it dove toward the other bed. I felt cold sweat pour down my face.

I could just make out the shape of a head on the pillow, an arm reaching for the bell on the wall. I thought I heard it ring. Moments later, hurried footsteps came down the hall, and someone knocked on my door.

"Monsieur's whisky," said a voice outside. "Sorry, monsieur. I brought it as fast as I could."

I was frozen. I couldn't speak. The knocking continued.

"Monsieur's whisky," he repeated.

At last, I forced my voice to work. I heard myself croak, "For God's sake, come in. I'm alone with it."

The door handle turned, and suddenly the lights came back on.

A waiter peeked into the room. But I didn't look at him—I was staring at the other bed.

A man lay there, his skin pale and sunken. His throat had been cut from ear to ear. Blood soaked the pillow and sheet.

Then, as if someone had flicked off a switch, the image vanished. Only the waiter remained, sleepy but clearly shaken.

"Monsieur rang?" he asked.

"No," I said. "But I won't sleep here tonight." And I made up a bed for myself in the billiard room.

The Thing in the Hall

What you're about to read is what Dr. Assheton told me about the Thing in the Hall. I wrote down everything as quickly as I could while he spoke, then later typed it up into a full story. I read it back to him the day before he died—probably within an hour of his death. Some of you might remember this from the coroner's inquest, where I had to testify. Just a week earlier, Dr. Assheton had done the same for his friend Louis Fielder, who died in exactly the same strange way. Back then, he gave his expert opinion as a brain doctor and said Louis had taken his own life while not in his right mind. That's also what the jury decided. But in Dr. Assheton's own case, even though the final verdict was the same, people weren't as sure.

I had to explain that right before he died, I read this whole story to him. He corrected a few small details very clearly and calmly. At the end, he said:

"I'm absolutely sure, as a brain specialist, that I am completely sane, and that everything I described really happened—not just in my imagination, but in real life. If I had to speak again about poor Louis, I would have to say something very different now. Please add that to your story—either at the end or the beginning, wherever it fits better."

Before you read the rest, I need to explain a few things. Dr. Francis Assheton and Louis Fielder met at Cambridge and were close friends up until they died. They were very different in personality. Dr. Assheton was calm and hardworking, and had already become a top expert on the brain by age 35. Louis was bright and full of big ideas, but never really focused on one thing long enough to finish it. He jumped from one project to the next—X-rays one week, flying machines the next, then spiritualism. But they shared one big thing: a deep curiosity about the unknown. That curiosity made them fearless, at least until the end.

Dr. Assheton once sat by a man dying from the plague just to study how the disease affected the brain. Louis would dive into any wild new idea just for the thrill of it. That shared hunger for understanding tied them together. The rest of this story is what Dr. Assheton told me. It's written in his words.

"After I got back from studying with Dr. Charcot in Paris, I started working as a doctor in London. People had begun accepting the idea of hypnotism and suggestion as ways to treat illness. I had written a few papers on the subject, and I had my degrees from France, so I got a lot of patients right away.

Louis had strong opinions about where I should live. He told me not to move to 'Chloroform Square'—his nickname for the part of town where most doctors lived—but instead to move to Chelsea, next to his own house.

'Who cares where a doctor lives,' he said, 'as long as he helps people get better? You don't believe in old-fashioned medicine—why live in an old-fashioned neighborhood? That place smells like quiet death. Come here and help people live! Besides, I'll want to tell you things almost every evening, and I can't come all the way across London to do that.'

When you've been gone for five years, it means a lot to have a close friend still nearby. And having Louis living next door sounded perfect. I remembered how he used to drop by at night when we were at Cambridge. As soon as I finished my work for the day, I'd hear his fast footsteps on the stairs, and then for hours he'd fill the room with new ideas. Being around him felt like feeding your brain—and I believed that's what kept people healthy.

Most people, I think, get sick because their minds are tired or empty. That stress shows up in the body as things like back pain or even cancer. That's the heart of my work. The brain needs food, rest, and exercise just like the body does. If you take care of the brain, the body stays well too. Medicines don't help if the brain is what's really sick—unless the person truly believes in them.

I remember telling Louis something like that one night when I had dinner at his house. Afterward, we sat down for coffee in what he called his 'hall.' His house looked just like mine on the outside—just another small London home—but inside, he had knocked down all the walls on the ground floor. Instead of separate rooms for dining, studying, and a hallway, he had one big open space. It made the house feel alive and welcoming. But there was one downside—you could hear everything, including the postman banging on the door.

Just as I finished explaining my theory about the brain and health, there was a loud knock that made me jump.

'You should cover your door knocker,' I said. 'At least during dinner.'

Louis laughed and leaned back in his chair.

'There isn't a knocker,' he said. 'You said the same thing last week. So I took it off. Now the letters just slide in through the slot. But you still heard a knock, didn't you?'

'Didn't you?' I asked.

'Of course I did. But it wasn't the postman. That's the Thing. I don't know what it is. That's what makes it so fascinating.'

Now, if there's one thing that people like me—hypnotists and brain doctors—can't stand, it's spiritualism. It goes against everything we believe. To us, it makes no more sense than thinking spirits can move furniture or change someone's fate. It's just as silly as giving someone a magic potion to make them smarter.

But that's what I believed back then."

I was sure it was the postman, so I got up and went to the door. There were no letters in the box, but when I opened the door, the postman was just walking up the steps. He handed me the mail.

When I got back, Louis was sipping his coffee.

"Have you ever tried table-turning?" he asked. "It's kind of strange."

"No, and I haven't tried rubbing violet leaves on cancer either," I said.

"Oh, come on, try everything," he replied. "That's always been your style—just like me. You've spent all these years testing new things—at first without believing, then with a little belief, and finally like you believed anything was possible. Remember? You didn't even believe in hypnotism when you first went to Paris."

He rang for his servant, who came and cleared the table. While that was happening, we wandered around the room looking at prints. Louis had bought a Bartolozzi that we both admired, but we stayed quiet over a 'Perdita' he'd paid a lot for. Then he sat back down at the dining table. It was round and heavy, made of dark wood, with one thick leg ending in clawed feet.

"Try pushing it," he said. "See how heavy it is."

I grabbed the edge and found I could barely move it. It was really solid.

"Now just place your hands lightly on top," he said. "Let's see what happens."

Nothing happened. My fingers just slid over the surface. I rolled my eyes at the idea of wasting the evening like this.

"I'd rather play chess or tic-tac-toe," I said. "Or even talk about politics. We'll both say we aren't pushing—but we'll end up doing it without meaning to."

Louis nodded. "Just for a moment," he said. "Let's both press as hard as we can from right to left with just our fingertips."

We pushed. At least, I did, and I saw his fingernails turn from pink to white from pressure, so he was pushing too. The table groaned once, but didn't move.

Then there was a sharp knock—not at the front door, but somewhere inside the room.

"It's the Thing," Louis said.

Looking back now, I suppose it really was. But at the time, it just felt like a challenge. I wanted to prove how silly it was.

"For five years now, on and off, I've been studying spiritualism," Louis said. "I never told you, because I wanted to show you things I can't explain—but that seem to happen when I try. You can see and hear them, and decide if you want to help."

"And to help me 'see better,' you're going to turn off the lights?" I asked.

"Yes. You'll understand why."

"I'm here as a skeptic," I reminded him.

"Then keep on skepticking," he said with a grin.

The room went dark, except for the faint glow of the fireplace. The thick curtains blocked out any streetlight, and the usual evening sounds from outside were muffled. I sat on one side of the table, near the door; Louis sat opposite, and I could just make out his outline against the firelight.

"Put your hands lightly on the table," he said. "And just… expect something."

I didn't believe it, but I followed his instructions. I could hear his breathing grow a little faster. I thought it was strange to get excited just standing in the dark, waiting around a table.

Then I felt something—just the tiniest vibration under my fingers, like when a kettle starts to boil. The shaking grew stronger, until it reminded me of a car engine rumbling. I thought I could hear a faint humming noise.

Then suddenly, the table started to turn slowly.

"Keep your hands on it and move with it," Louis said. I saw his outline shift away from the fire as he followed the table's movement.

We circled the table for a bit in silence, shuffling along as it moved. Then Louis spoke again, his voice trembling.

"Are you there?" he asked.

No answer.

He asked again. This time, a loud knock came, like the one I'd heard earlier and thought was the postman. But this time, it sounded much louder. It didn't seem to come from one place—it filled the room.

The table stopped turning, but it kept shaking. I stared at it, though I couldn't see much in the dark. Suddenly, a small spark of light flashed across the table—I saw my hands for just a second. Then another flash came, and another, like someone striking matches in the dark or like fireflies floating through a summer garden.

Then came a deafening knock, and the table stopped shaking. The little sparks of light disappeared.

That was what happened at the first séance I ever attended. But I should point out that Fielder had been practicing what he called "expecting" for several years. If we use spiritualist terms—though I didn't believe in them back then—he was the medium and I was just an observer. Everything I saw that night, he had either experienced before or could make happen regularly. I say that because he told me some of the things now seemed to happen without him doing anything. The knocking sounds would happen even when he wasn't thinking about them, and sometimes they woke him up while he was asleep. The lights, too, appeared without him trying to cause them.

At the time, I believed all of it came from inside his own mind. When he said he couldn't control it, I thought he meant it had sunk into his unconscious—into the part of the mind we don't fully understand, but which plays a huge role in our lives. In fact, most of what we do seems to come from that part of us. We don't choose to hear or see—it just happens. We don't really think about walking or moving; it's automatic. Even when we learn something new like skating, at first it's hard. But once we've got the hang of it, we stop thinking about it—just like walking.

As someone who studied the brain, I found this all incredibly interesting. And as someone who studied hypnotism, it was even more fascinating. What I believed that night was this: everything I saw and heard, I only experienced because Louis did. It was an amazing example of thought-transference. His ideas were so strong that I picked them up—so clearly that I saw and heard things that were only happening in his mind.

Later, we talked about what happened. Louis believed the Thing was trying to talk to us. He thought it was what moved the table, made the tapping sounds, and created the flashes of light.

"But this Thing," I said, cutting in, "what are you talking about? Some long-dead uncle? I've seen enough séances where a relative shows up and says boring, pointless stuff. Or is it some kind of spirit? Whose spirit?"

Louis sat across from me, the small table lamp lighting his face. I saw his eyes suddenly widen. As a doctor, I knew that meant fear—unless the light had changed, which it hadn't. A moment later, his eyes went back to normal.

He stood up and faced the fireplace.

"No, I don't think it's anyone's uncle," he said. "Like I told you before, I don't know what the Thing is. But if you really want to know what I think, I believe it's an Elemental."

"What's an Elemental?" I asked.

Again, his eyes widened.

"I can explain it in two minutes," he said. "Listen—there are good things in the world, right? And there are bad things too. Cancer is bad. Fresh air is good. Honesty is good. Lying is bad. Some kind of force pushes people to do both good and bad things. And some kind of power suggests those urges. When I started all this spiritual stuff, I was neutral. I opened myself up and said, 'Anyone can come in.' And now I think something has taken me up on that offer. The Thing you saw—the one that knocked, moved the table, and sparked lights across it—I believe that was it.

"I think there's a force behind the evil in the world, and that it sends messengers to do its work. I call those messengers Elementals. People have seen them before. I'm sure they'll be seen again. I never asked for good spirits to visit. I don't want some ghost to show up and play hymns on a music box. But I didn't ask for an Elemental either. All I did was open the door. I think the Thing is now in my house, and it's trying to communicate with me.

"And I want to know what it is. I want to know the truth—even if it's something evil. Even if it comes from Satan himself. I just want to know."

What happened next could easily have been my imagination, but this is what I believed actually happened. There was a piano near the door with sheet music on it, and suddenly a strong gust of wind blew through the room. The music pages rustled, a vase of daffodils shook, and their yellow petals nodded. The wind reached the candles near us, making their flames flicker low and blue. Then I felt the breeze hit me—it was cold and moved my hair. It swirled across to Louis, and I saw his hair shift too. Finally, it moved toward the fireplace, and the flames flared up as if blown by a gust. The rug by the fire even lifted.

"That was weird, wasn't it?" Louis said.

"So, has your Elemental gone up the chimney?" I asked.

"Oh no," he replied. "It just passed by us."

Then he suddenly pointed to the wall just behind my chair, and his voice cracked.

"Look! What's that?" he said. "Right there on the wall."

Startled, I turned in the direction he was pointing. The wall was light gray, and there was a sharp shadow on it. As I stared, it moved. It looked like a giant slug—fat, without legs, about two feet tall and four feet long. At one end, it had a head like a seal's, with its mouth open and tongue hanging out.

Then it faded. Right after that, we heard another loud bang, just like before.

For a moment, we sat in silence. The room felt thick with fear, like heavy snow in the air. But surprisingly, neither of us stayed scared for long. The whole thing was just too fascinating.

"That's what I meant when I said I couldn't control it," Louis said. "I told you I was open to anything coming in—and wow, did we get something intense."

Even after seeing that creepy shadow, I still believed this was just a strange case of brain disorder, with really powerful thought-sharing. I didn't think I saw a monster—I thought Louis imagined it so strongly that I picked it up too. I later noticed that the spiritual books he read—books I called junk—said this slug shape was a common form for Elementals. Louis, on the other hand, believed more than ever that what we experienced was real and not just in our minds.

Over the next six months, we kept doing séances, but nothing new happened. The shadow didn't return, and the Thing didn't show up again. I started to feel like we were wasting our time. Then I had an idea. We'd bring in a medium, put him under hypnosis, and see if that revealed anything new. So we gathered around the dining-room table again. The room was dim, but I could still see clearly.

The medium, a young man, sat between Louis and me. It was easy to put him into a light hypnotic sleep. Immediately, loud knocking sounds started, and something with a faint glow slid across the table. It wasn't just a shadow—it looked like it was faintly glowing, like something slowly burning. At the same time, the medium's face twisted in total terror. His eyes and mouth were wide open, staring at something near him. The Thing moved closer, reaching for his throat. With a terrified scream, the medium jumped up, trying to push it away. But whatever it was had already grabbed him, and he couldn't break free.

Louis and I rushed to help. My hands touched something cold and slimy, but we couldn't pull it off him. It was like trying to grab wet fur—it slipped through our fingers and felt disgusting, like touching rotting flesh. Desperate and still not believing this was real, I remembered that the light switch was close by. I turned on all four electric lights.

There was the medium on the floor, with Louis kneeling beside him, looking pale and shaken. But the Thing was gone. Only the medium's shirt collar was torn, and there were two bleeding scratches on his neck.

He was still under hypnosis, so I woke him up. He touched his collar and throat, feeling the blood, but, as expected, he didn't remember anything. We told him something unusual had happened and that he had struggled with it in his sleep. We said he had helped us, and we were grateful.

I never saw him again. A week later, he died from blood poisoning.

That night marked the beginning of the next phase of this story. The Thing had become physical. The massive slug-like Elemental wasn't just tapping or moving furniture anymore. Now it had a body—one that could be seen and touched. But still, I kept telling myself that it only appeared in half-light. When I turned on the lights, nothing was there. Maybe the medium had grabbed his own neck. Maybe Louis and I had just touched each other in panic. I said these things to calm myself, but deep down, I didn't believe them as firmly as I believed the sun would rise the next day.

As a brain specialist and student of hypnosis, I should've kept studying what happened. But I had work, and I found it impossible to focus on anything else. The events next door haunted me, so I stopped going to séances with Louis.

I had another reason, too. In those last four or five months, Louis changed. He became cruel and immoral. I've never been a saint myself, but Louis was becoming horrible. He was kicked out of a club for cheating at cards and told me about it proudly. He tortured his cat. He turned into someone disgusting. I used to feel sick walking past his house, scared of what might look back at me from the window.

Then, just a week ago, I was woken in the night by a terrible scream—long, rising and falling. It came from Louis' house. I ran downstairs in my pajamas and into the street. A policeman had heard it too. It was coming from Louis' hallway. The window was open. We broke the door down together. You know what we found. The screaming had stopped just moments before. But Louis was already dead. Both sides of his neck had been torn open.

It was early morning when I returned to my house. As I walked in, I felt something soft and slimy brush past me. This time it couldn't have been Louis' imagination.

Since then, I've seen flickers of the Thing every night. It wakes me up with tapping sounds, and in the dark corners of my room, I can see something sitting there—something more solid than just a shadow.

Less than an hour after I left Dr. Assheton, the quiet street was filled again with terrible screams. By the time they got into the house, he was already dead—killed in the same awful way as his friend.

The House with the Brick-Kiln

The small village of Trevor Major is hidden in a quiet valley on the north side of the South Downs, west of Lewes, and runs along the coast. It only has about thirty or forty small houses and cottages, surrounded by trees. But the large old church and the big manor house just outside the village show that the place used to be more important. The manor house has been empty since the summer of 1896, except for a short stay by renters nearly four years ago. Even though the rent is super cheap, I doubt anyone would want to stay there again—not even in hard times. I was one of those renters, and I'd rather live in a crowded workhouse than spend another night in that dark, old place. I'd even prefer looking out at the dirty streets of Whitechapel than staring at the quiet woods and clear stream by the manor, where trout swim in the cool water and plants wave under the surface.

Jack Singleton and I rented the house because we heard there were trout in the stream. We planned to stay for a month from mid-May to mid-June, but we left after just three weeks. Still, we had our best day of fishing on the last afternoon. Jack had seen the house in a Sussex newspaper that said it came with great dry-fly fishing. We didn't believe it at first because we'd been fooled before, visiting places that promised good fishing but had nothing. But after walking by the stream for half an hour, we went straight to the agent and rented it right away.

We got there from London around five in the afternoon on a sunny day in May. Even though I now remember what happened later with fear, I still can't forget how beautiful it all looked when we arrived. The garden hadn't been taken care of for years. Weeds filled the gravel paths, and the flowerbeds were a mix of wild and planted flowers. The garden was surrounded by an old brick wall, with little flowers growing in the cracks. Behind that was a circle of tall pine trees, and the wind made them sound like the sea. Beyond that, the ground sloped down to a stream that curved around three sides of the garden and flowed through two large fields that led to the village. We had the right to fish all along that part of the stream, even a quarter mile upstream to a stone bridge near the road that led to the house. On the last side of the house, up a little hill, there was an old brick-kiln falling apart. Nearby was a shallow pit covered in tall grass and wildflowers, where they used to dig for clay.

The house was long and narrow. When you walked in, you were in a square hall with wooden walls. On the left was the dining room, which led to the kitchen and other back rooms. On the right were two sitting rooms—one looked out at the driveway, the other at the garden. From the first one, you could see the brick-kiln through the trees. A wooden staircase led up from the hall to a hallway above, with three main bedrooms. A narrow hallway with a red curtain at the end led to two guest rooms and the servants' area.

Jack and I shared a flat in London, and we had sent our longtime servants, Franklyn and his wife, ahead to prepare the house. Mrs. Franklyn greeted us with a big smile. She was used to the bad conditions in fishing houses but was happy with what she found. The kitchen worked well, and both hot and cold water came out of the taps without problems. Her husband had gone to the village to get supplies. She brought us tea and then went upstairs to unpack our bags. We chose two bedrooms—one above the dining room and one above the larger sitting room. The doors were right across from each other. Jack's room had a smaller, empty room next to it that opened from his.

Before dinner, we went fishing for a couple of hours and each caught several trout. When we got back, Franklyn said he'd found a woman from the village to come help in the mornings. He also said people in the village seemed surprised we were staying in the manor. Many asked if we really planned to live there. When he said yes, they just went quiet and shook their heads. But Sussex people are known for being quiet and not very friendly, so we didn't worry about it.

The evening was warm and peaceful. After dinner, we brought chairs outside and sat in front of the house while it got darker. The moon hadn't risen yet, and the trees blocked most of the starlight, so it was very dark. When we went inside, drawn by the light in the sitting room, I suddenly felt something strange—like something scary and invisible was near me. Even though it was warm, I shivered. I didn't tell Jack, but I followed him into the smaller sitting room, which we hadn't used yet.

That room also had wooden walls, and hanging on them were six watercolor paintings. At first, we looked at them without much interest, but then we noticed how detailed they were. Each painting showed a part of the house or garden. One showed a sunset through the trees. Another showed the garden in the heat of summer. Another had storm clouds over the field and stream. The most detailed one showed the old brick-kiln. It was the only painting with a person in it—a man in grey clothes standing at the kiln's open door, with a red light glowing inside. He was painted very clearly, with a sharp nose and a square chin. The tall, narrow painting showed the chimney with smoke drifting into the dark sky.

Jack stared at the painting for a moment.

"That's a creepy picture," he said. "But it's painted so well. It feels like it's showing something real, not just a random scene. Like it really happened. By Jove—"

He stopped mid-sentence and quickly looked at the other paintings one by one.

"That's strange," he said. "Do you see what I see?"

Since the image of the brick-kiln was fresh in my mind, it wasn't hard to spot what he meant. In every single painting, the brick-kiln was there—sometimes partly hidden behind trees, sometimes in full view—but always with smoke coming out of the chimney.

"What's strange is that you can't even see the kiln from the garden," Jack added. "The house blocks it. But the artist, someone with the initials F.A., keeps showing it."

"What do you think it means?" I asked.

"No idea. Maybe he just really liked painting brick-kilns. Let's play some cards."

Two weeks of our three-week stay went by without anything major happening, except that I kept getting this weird, heavy feeling like something awful was nearby. I sort of got used to it, but at the same time, it started to feel even stronger. One night near the end of the second week, I finally brought it up to Jack.

"That's weird. I've felt that too," he said. "When does it hit you? Do you feel it now?"

We were sitting outside after dinner again, and as he spoke, the feeling hit me harder than ever. At that exact moment, the front door—which had been closed, though maybe not latched—slowly swung open. A strip of light from the hallway shone out for a second before the door slowly swung shut again, like something had quietly slipped inside.

"Yes," I said. "I felt it just now. It always happens in the evening. That one felt worse than usual."

Jack was quiet for a moment.

"It's strange, that door opening and closing like that," he said. "Let's go inside."

We got up, and I noticed the windows of my bedroom were lit—Mrs. Franklyn was probably getting things ready for bed. As we crossed the gravel, we suddenly heard fast footsteps on the stairs. When we walked in, Mrs. Franklyn was standing in the hall looking pale and shocked.

"Is something wrong?" I asked.

She took a few deep breaths before answering.

"No, sir. At least, not something I can explain. I was tidying your room and thought I saw you walk in. But nobody was there, and it gave me a scare. I left my candle—I need to go back for it."

I waited in the hall while she went upstairs and walked down the hallway to my room. The door was open, and she stopped in the doorway without going in.

"What is it?" I called up.

"I left the candle burning," she said, "but it's gone out."

Jack chuckled.

"And you left the window and door open," he said.

"Yes, sir—but there's no wind at all," she said softly.

She was right. The air was still, yet the heavy front door had moved on its own just moments ago. Jack ran upstairs.

"Don't worry, Mrs. Franklyn. I'll go with you," he said.

He entered my room, and I heard him strike a match. Light from the candle glowed through the open door. At the same time, we heard a bell ring in the servants' area. A moment later, footsteps came, and Franklyn appeared.

"Which bell was that?" I asked.

"Mr. Jack's room, sir," he said.

The whole house suddenly felt on edge, even though nothing truly frightening had happened. Mrs. Franklyn thought I had entered my room, but I hadn't. Then her candle went out—probably because of a draft. The bell ringing, if it really did ring, wasn't a big deal.

"Probably just a mouse brushing the wire," I said. "Mr. Jack is up there right now, lighting her candle."

Jack came back down, and we went to the sitting room. But Franklyn didn't seem convinced. We could hear his heavy footsteps upstairs in Jack's room. Then we heard him walk into the next room, and after that, everything went quiet.

I was unusually sleepy that night and went to bed earlier than usual. My sleep was restless—I'd fall into a deep sleep and then wake up suddenly, fully alert. Sometimes the house was completely silent, with only the wind in the pine trees. Other times, it felt like the house was full of quiet, strange movements. Once, I could have sworn I heard the doorknob turning. I had to check. I lit my candle, but the handle hadn't moved. Still, I thought I heard footsteps outside. Nervously, I opened the door, but the hallway was empty and still. Then I heard snoring from Jack's room across the hall, which made me feel better. I went back to bed and finally slept peacefully. When I woke again, the sky was turning red with morning light, and the fear I'd felt all night was gone.

The next day, heavy rain started after lunch. Since the water was muddy and rising, and I had letters to write, I left Jack fishing by the stream and came back around five. I spent a couple of hours writing at a desk in the front room—the one with the paintings. By seven, I was done, and as I got up to light the candles, I thought I saw Jack coming out of the bushes near the path to the stream.

But then I felt a sudden chill—something wasn't right. It wasn't Jack. It was someone I didn't know. He was only about six yards from the window. After pausing, he walked right up to the glass and stared in at me. The light from the candles lit up his face clearly. I didn't recognize him, but something about him looked familiar. He smiled, but it wasn't a friendly smile—it was cold and cruel. Then, without a word, he walked toward the front door and out of sight.

Even though I didn't like the man's appearance, there was something about him that seemed familiar. He looked like he was heading toward the front door, so I walked into the hallway to meet him and see what he wanted. I opened the door before he could knock, expecting to find him standing there. But the gravel path outside was empty. Rain was pouring down, and it was getting dark. As I stood there, I felt something I couldn't see slide past me and enter the house. Then the stairs creaked, and a moment later, a bell rang.

Franklyn, always quick to respond, hurried past me and went upstairs. He knocked on Jack's door, went inside for a moment, then came back down.

"Is Mr. Jack still out, sir?" he asked.

"Yes. Was that his bell again?"

"Yes, sir," he said calmly.

I returned to the sitting room. Soon, Franklyn brought in a lamp and set it under the painting of the brick-kiln. As I looked at it, I suddenly realized why the man outside had looked so familiar—he was exactly like the figure in the painting. It wasn't just a similarity. It was the same person. But who was he? And what exactly came into the house when I opened the door?

Right then, I felt a wave of fear I'd never experienced before. My mouth went dry, and my heart thudded painfully in my chest. This wasn't just nervousness or a creepy feeling—it was pure, cold fear. Still, even though nothing happened to calm me down, the feeling faded. I tried to think logically. I had seen someone outside. Maybe he just walked past the door and continued down the road. Maybe I only imagined that something came in. And the bell? That had gone off randomly before. I kept telling myself these things until I believed them enough to settle down. I wasn't exactly at ease, but I wasn't panicking anymore.

I sat near the window and found another letter to read. Outside, the driveway stretched through a gap in the pine trees and into the field with the brick-kiln. While flipping pages, I looked up and noticed something odd. At the same time, I smelled something—something like roasted meat. I saw smoke rising from the chimney of the brick-kiln. The light breeze was blowing from the kiln toward the house. I told myself the smell probably came from the kitchen, where dinner was being made. I needed to believe that so I wouldn't fall back into fear.

Then I heard footsteps on the gravel path and the rattle of the front door. Jack walked in.

"Great fishing," he said. "You gave up too early."

He walked straight to the painting of the brick-kiln and stared at it. There was a long silence before I finally asked him something I needed to know.

"Did you see anyone?"

"Yes. Why?"

"Because I did too—the man in that painting."

Jack came and sat down beside me.

"He's a ghost," he said. "He showed up at the river around sunset and stood nearby for almost an hour. At first, I thought he was just a man and told him to step back so he wouldn't get hooked. Then I realized he wasn't real. I even cast my line right through him. Around seven, he headed up toward the house."

"Were you scared?"

"No. It was actually really fascinating. So, you saw him too? Where was he?"

"Just outside. I think he's inside the house now."

Jack looked around the room.

"Did you see him come in?" he asked.

"No, but I felt him. Also, the chimney of the brick-kiln is smoking."

Jack looked out the window. It was nearly dark, but the curling smoke was still visible.

"You're right," he said. "It's thick and greasy. I'm going to check it out. Want to come?"

"I'll stay here," I said.

"Afraid? It's not scary—it's just incredibly interesting."

Jack came back from the kiln still curious. He didn't see anyone, but even in the low light, he saw a faint glow inside the kiln. Against the dark sky, thick white smoke floated upward. The rest of the night was quiet, and the next day passed without anything strange.

But that calm didn't last.

That night, while I was changing for bed, I heard a bell ring loudly. I also thought I heard someone yell. Since Franklyn and his wife had already gone to sleep, I figured it was Jack's bell and went straight to his room. Just as I was about to knock, I heard his voice from inside.

"Be careful! He's right outside the door!"

I was hit with a sudden wave of fear, but I forced myself to stay calm. I opened the door, and again, something I couldn't see brushed past me and slipped out. Nothing was visible.

Jack stood next to his bed, half-dressed, wiping sweat from his forehead.

"He came back," Jack said. "I was standing here when I suddenly felt him right next to me. I think he came from the other room. Did you see what he was holding?"

"No, I didn't see anything," I said.

"It was a knife. A big carving knife. Can I sleep on your couch tonight? That really scared me. There was something else too. At the edges of his clothes—his collar and wrists—there were small white flames, just flickering like they were alive."

The next day passed quietly. We didn't see or hear anything unusual, and even that night, the heavy feeling that something awful was in the house didn't return. Then came our final day there. We had stayed out until after dark and had an amazing time fishing. When we got home, we were sitting together in the living room when suddenly, from upstairs, we heard footsteps, the loud ringing of a bell, and then screams—terrible, painful screams like someone was being attacked.

We both instantly thought it might be Mrs. Franklyn, terrified by something awful, and we ran upstairs and burst into Jack's room.

The door to the next room was open, and just inside, we saw the man bending over something dark and crumpled on the floor. Even though the room was dim, we could see him clearly. It was like a faint, sickly light was coming from his body. He had the long knife in his hand again, and as we stepped in, he was wiping it on the figure at his feet. Then he picked it up, and we saw it was a woman—her head nearly cut off.

But it wasn't Mrs. Franklyn.

Then everything disappeared. The man, the body, the light—it was all gone. We stood in the doorway staring into an empty, dark room. We went downstairs without saying a word. It wasn't until we were back in the sitting room that Jack finally spoke.

"He takes her to the brick-kiln," he said, his voice shaking. "I don't know about you, but I'm done with this place. There's something evil in it."

About a week later, Jack handed me a Sussex guidebook. It was open to the page about Trevor Major. I read:

"Just outside the village is the old manor house, once home to the artist and well-known murderer Francis Adam. He killed his wife here, supposedly in a jealous rage, by cutting her throat. He then burned her body in a brick-kiln. Some burned remains were found six months later, which led to his arrest and execution."

So I've decided to leave the house—with its brick-kiln and the paintings signed F.A.—to someone else.

The End

Thank You for Reading

Dear Reader,

We hope this timeless classic has sparked your imagination and enriched your literary journey. Now that you've turned the final page, we want to share a vision for the future of reading—one where every classic you've ever wanted to explore is at your fingertips, in a format that best suits your life.

We'd like to invite you to gain immediate, unlimited digital & audiobook access to hundreds of the most treasured literary classics ever written—along with the option to secure deluxe paperback, hardcover & box set editions at printing cost. Together, we can spark a new global literary renaissance alongside our small, independent publishing house called "The Library of Alexandria."

Thousands of years ago, the Library of Alexandria stood as a beacon of knowledge—until it was lost to history. We aim to reignite that spirit of preservation and discovery right now, in the modern age—only this time, it's accessible to all, in every language and every format.

Picture a world where every timeless classic, novel, poem, or philosophical treatise is not only available to read but also updated for today's readers—modernized, translated into any language or dialect, and ready to enjoy in any format you choose, whether that is in an eBook, audiobook, paperback, or deluxe hardcover & box set version a printing cost.

By joining our movement to rebuild the modern Library of Alexandria, you become part of an unprecedented mission to offer:

- **Unlimited Audiobook & eBook Access to the Greatest Classics of All Time**

  Instantly explore thousands of legendary works, from Plato and Shakespeare to Jane Austen and Leo Tolstoy. All are instantly ready to read or listen to, giving you a complete literary universe at your fingertips.

- **Paperback & Deluxe Editions at Printing Costs:**

  Purchase any title in a paperback, deluxe hardbound, or deluxe boxset edition at printing costs, shipped right to your doorstep. Curate your personal library of Alexandria with editions worthy of display—crafted to last, designed to captivate, and delivered straight to your door.

- **Modern translations for Contemporary Readers in all languages and dialects**

  Discover a vast selection of classics reimagined in clear, current language—no more struggling with outdated phrases or obscure references. Next to the original versions, we aim to offer translations in as many languages and dialects as possible.

  As we continue our translation efforts and add new languages, readers everywhere can connect with these works as if they were written today. By bridging linguistic divides, you're contributing to ensuring that these timeless stories become more meaningful, accessible, and inspiring for people across the globe.

- **Your Personal Library of Alexandria:**

  Over the months and years, you'll curate a unique physical archive of classics—each volume a testament to your taste, curiosity, and love of knowledge. It's not just about owning books—it's about curating a cultural legacy you'll cherish and pass down for generations to come.

- **Join a Global Literary Renaissance:**

  Your support fuels an ongoing mission: allowing us to reinvest in offering deluxe print editions (including special boxsets) at their true cost, broaden the range of available formats and translations, and extend the reach of these works to new audiences worldwide. By joining today, you're not just preserving a legacy of masterpieces; you set in motion a powerful wave of literary accessibility.

  We are more than a publisher—we're a movement, and we can't do it alone. Your support lets us scale our mission, preserving and reimagining history's greatest works for tomorrow's readers.

Become a Torchbearer of knowledge.

Thank you for picking up this book and allowing us into your literary journey. As you turn the pages, know that you're part of something larger: a global effort to keep these stories alive, share their wisdom across borders and generations, and spark a true cultural revival for the modern era.

If this resonates with you—please consider taking the next step by visiting:

www.libraryofalexandria.com

With gratitude and a shared love of knowledge,

The Modern Library of Alexandria Team

Visit:

www.libraryofalexandria.com

Or scan the code below: